LOVING TEXAS TEA

A Sweet Romance

Billionaire's Bet

Book 2

A.B. PROEBSTEL

ISBN-13: 978-1-946292-34-6

ISBN-10: 1-946292-34-6

Printed in the United States of America

First Printing, 2019

Second Printing, 2022

Third Printing, 2023

Website: https://geni.us/LOA-Home
BookBub: https://geni.us/BBFollow
Goodreads: www.goodreads.com/aproebstel
Facebook: https://geni.us/FB-LOA
X: https://geni.us/Amy-T
Instagram: www.instagram.com/amyproebstel

BOOKS IN THE BILLIONAIRE'S BET SERIES

Book Zero: A Billionaire's Patent for Love

Book One: A Cowboy's Recipe for Romance

Book Two: Loving Texas Tea

Book Three: Properties of Love

Book Four: Plane Love

Book Five: Capitalizing on Love

Book Six: An Unleashed Love

Book Seven: Ether of Love

DEDICATION

First of all, this book is dedicated to my friends and family. Your support in helping me carve out time to write and your encouragement to keep me going even when life got in the way, has been utterly amazing. I've been so inspired by your thoughtfulness and I hope it shows in my writing.

Secondly, to the readers of this series, I greatly appreciate all of your kind words, amazing reviews, and support along the way. None of this would be possible without your enthusiasm for the characters and their stories.

CHAPTER 1

REGGIE

The newspaper lay open on Reggie's desk, and he found himself unable to tear his eyes away from Bethany's picture. It had been years since he last saw her, but her beauty still had a hold on him.

He tried to push aside the memories of their fifth-grade incident, but they kept resurfacing, reminding him of the hurt and embarrassment he had experienced. Too bad she was a black widow in disguise.

The headline only fueled his suspicions, "Prominent Woman Stands Up Her Groom At the Altar." He couldn't help but wonder if she was up to her old tricks again.

Against his better judgment, he leaned back in his plush office chair, giving in to the temptation to read the salacious details.

Just as he was getting absorbed in the article, a knock sounded on his office door, jolting him back to reality. He dropped the newspaper onto his desk guiltily and called out, "Come in!"

The petite, blonde administrative assistant, Shannon, poked her head through the doorway. "Your staff is waiting for you in the conference room. Can I get you anything?"

Reggie snapped back to the present and glanced at the digital clock on the corner of his computer. He mentally scolded himself for being five minutes late to the meeting he had called himself. Shoving the offending newspaper aside, he grabbed the folder of notes off his desk and stood to leave.

Once again, Bethany had managed to disrupt his day. Although she unknowingly did it this time, it was still her fault. Suppressing the old hurt, he nodded his head curtly as he passed Shannon at the doorway, ready to face the challenges of the day ahead.

"I think we should have bagels and donuts brought in for this meeting. I've got a feeling we're going to be a while," Reggie suggested, trying to refocus his attention on the matter at hand.

"Sure thing, boss." Shannon turned away, her pencil skirt emphasizing her graceful movements as she walked back to her desk.

Reggie couldn't help but appreciate the view for a moment longer than was strictly professional before snapping himself back to reality. He couldn't afford any distractions, especially not with thoughts of Bethany resurfacing. It would never do for him to seek any type of relationship with his long-time secretary, but it sure was tempting.

Entering the meeting in progress, Reggie was relieved to see his right-hand man, Adam, had taken the lead. As he had groomed him to do, Adam had initiated the meeting with an introduction to their plans for expansion. Choosing a seat in the back, Reggie watched over the group with a keen eye.

However, even Adam's proficiency couldn't fully engage Reggie's wandering mind. The image of Bethany Miller lingered. She was more beautiful than he remembered, and he found himself pondering the idea of reaching out to her, maybe to play a trick or two.

He shook his head, dismissing the notion as beneath him. He had more important things to focus on, like the party he was hosting over the weekend. Some of his most promising clients were attending, and he had invited a bevy of beautiful women from Texas to join in the festivities. Most definitely, his time would be spent entertaining and schmoozing the clients.

His mind was still entangled in thoughts of Bethany. He couldn't help but wonder if she was ready to step back into the social spotlight after the humiliating almost-wedding. The newspaper claimed they had "irreconcilable differences," but Reggie couldn't help but smirk at the notion. Of course, she would say such a thing. She probably did not like the suit he wore to the wedding and decided to call it off.

Lost in his musings, Reggie suddenly snapped back to reality as he noticed the room's silence. All eyes were on him, and he realized he had missed Adam's question. Clearing his throat, he stood and walked confidently to where Adam waited.

"Sorry about that, Adam. My mind was just, uh, processing some ideas," Reggie chuckled, hoping to brush off his momentary lapse. He took his place at the podium and gathered his thoughts back to the business at hand.

Yet, his mind kept wandering back to Bethany, like a song stuck on repeat. He hated feeling so out of sorts, but her article had undeniably stirred something in him. As he fumbled with the papers, he couldn't help but wonder how their paths would cross again and what impact it might have on his life.

"I gathered as much. I just mentioned that you wanted to present the potential client opportunities, and I called you up. The stage is yours," Adam replied, giving him a reassuring pat on the shoulder as he moved aside to take his seat in the front row.

Reggie stepped up to the podium, trying to shake off the lingering distraction of Bethany's article. He set his folder down and began organizing his thoughts back to the task at hand. Despite his best efforts, the vivid memories of his past with Bethany continued to swirl in his mind, making it difficult to focus.

Unconsciously, he picked up a paper and pretended to read it, using it as a cover to collect his thoughts. His employees could wait for him to be ready; after all, this was his meeting.

Taking a deep breath, Reggie finally looked up, feeling more composed. With determination, he began presenting potential client opportunities with confidence and flair. As he spoke, he couldn't help but marvel at how his past and present seemed to intersect in unexpected ways, and how Bethany's return had inadvertently affected his business decisions.

With each passing moment, the distractions faded into the background, and Reggie's focus returned to the matters at hand. He couldn't afford to let his personal life interfere with his professional endeavors, no matter how intriguing Bethany's reappearance might be.

As the meeting continued, Reggie made sure to keep his mind on track, navigating the world of oil industries with finesse and skill.

BETHANY

Fed up with the idea of spending the day as a sobbing mess in her hotel room, Bethany decided to take matters into her own hands. Sure, Pete might have acted like a first-class jerk and betrayed her with her own best friend the day before their wedding, but she wasn't going to let that be the final chapter of her story. No way!

Determined to seize the day, she picked up her phone and dialed her other bridesmaid's number. Lunch was calling, and she needed some fresh air ASAP. Plus, she had to escape the pitying gazes of the hotel staff. None of them knew what Pete had done to her, and if she had anything to say about it, they never would. It was just too humiliating.

As she waited for Shannon to answer, Bethany glanced at herself in the mirror. Well, her eyes were a tad puffy from the teary escapades of last night, but honestly, she didn't look half as terrible as she felt. Maybe there was a glimmer of hope that she could transform herself into a presentable human being in no time.

But then she noticed her old habit of biting her bottom lip resurfacing. Oh, the horror! It had been ages since she'd done that, back in the cringe-worthy days of high school. She shuddered at the memories, eager to leave that awkward phase far behind.

Ah, high school, where all the drama began. Those memories seemed to revolve around two people—Pete and Reggie. Back then, it was the dream relationship, with Bethany as the cheer captain and Pete as the football team's hero.

Everyone always said she and Pete were the perfect couple. Her class had nominated them as the King and Queen of Homecoming, where she felt like royalty sitting on the back of the Rolls Royce as they waved to the crowd waiting to watch the game. She had believed all the lies as well—until the wedding, that is.

Little did she know that those dreamy days would lead to such a nightmarish present.

Reggie, though... He was a whole other story. Now that she was an adult with better judgment (well, most of the time), she wanted nothing to do with him and his charming ways. Maybe it was for the best. High school romances rarely ended well, and hers had certainly gone up in flames—literally, with Pete's betrayal.

As the phone rang, Bethany prepared to leave the past where it belonged and step into a future that was free from drama and heartache. Today, she was taking control of her life, kicking aside the tears, and embracing the adventure that lay ahead. Who knows, maybe lunch with Shannon would be the start of something new and exciting.

With that thought, a spark of hope ignited within her, and a smile crept onto her face. Today, she was leaving behind the past, putting her high school days and the ghosts of exes in the rearview mirror. It was time for her to shine, and she was ready to make this unexpected turn of events into the best plot twist of her life.

Shannon's voice broke through her thoughts, and she stammered to recall why she had called in the first place. "Hey, Shannon! It's me, Bethany. I was wondering if you wanted to do lunch today. I mean, I know it's short notice and all, but—"

"Sure thing! Can you meet me in twenty minutes? The boss is holding a never-ending meeting, and I'm trying to sneak out early. I've got a feeling we'll be working late nights until this crazy new contract is buttoned up."

"Twenty minutes it is! Do you want me to pick you up at the office?" Panic set in as Bethany realized she wouldn't even have time for a shower, let alone a proper outfit selection. Her mind raced, hoping she could manage to look presentable in record time.

As she pulled up to the fancy office building where Shannon worked, the parking stars seemed to align. A prime spot opened up just for her tiny little sports car, and she took it as a sign of good things to come. "I got a spot right out front," she declared triumphantly over the phone.

"Lucky you! Unfortunately, I'm stuck here for a little while longer. Waiting on a food delivery, of all things. Why don't you come up and keep me company?"

Bethany agreed, ready to tackle any obstacle in her path to delicious food and much-needed girl talk. She navigated the busy street like a boss, making her way into the impressive building. The security guard at the lobby desk couldn't help but admire her confidence, and she couldn't blame him – she was looking pretty fabulous today.

At least she still had something after her ex shattered her confidence in men altogether. With a polite nod to the guard, she pressed on toward the elevator, determined to find Shannon's desk on the illustrious sixteenth floor. Her resolve to leave behind the pity party of last week's heartbreak was stronger than ever, and she couldn't wait to share her newfound boldness with her loyal friend.

Feeling a touch of sass in her step and enjoying the lingering attention of the guard, Bethany confidently waited for the elevator. As soon as the doors slid open, she gracefully stepped inside and pressed the button for the sixteenth floor. She couldn't help but smile at the idea of someone admiring her without any ulterior motives – unlike her ex, Pete, who turned out to be a real piece of work.

The elevator ride was surprisingly pleasant, and Bethany relished in the little moment of self-appreciation. She refused to let Pete's betrayal cloud her day any further. As the doors opened, she walked out and turned right, eager to find Shannon's desk.

However, much to her confusion, all she found was a glass wall with a sea of people sitting in an intense-looking meeting. The meeting was so official that she wondered if she had stepped into a boardroom scene from a movie. She looked around, hoping to spot Shannon somewhere amidst the crowd.

But instead, her gaze fell upon a charismatic man, dressed impeccably in a dark suit, captivating the entire room with his presence. For a moment, time seemed to freeze as their eyes locked. She was taken aback, and her cheeks flushed with warmth. In an instant, she recognized him as none other than her childhood nemesis, Reginald Bartholomew.

Her heart pounded, and she couldn't help but feel a mix of surprise and intrigue. There he was, her old rival from back in the day, looking all grown-up and commanding the room like a true CEO. Despite their past rivalry, she couldn't deny that he had an undeniable magnetism.

Reality snapped her back to her senses, and she quickly turned on her heel, trying to compose herself as she walked away. In her haste, she collided with a man exiting the elevator. Several packages teetered from the man's arms, falling in slow motion toward the floor. With practiced ease, Bethany swiped the falling bags up into her hands just shy of them landing. Flustered, she apologized with a nervous chuckle.

"Sorry about that! I didn't mean to barrel into you." She flashed a charming smile, hoping to brush off the awkward encounter.

Bethany felt the weight of Reggie's stare on her back, adding another layer of discomfort to her already embarrassing encounter. Why did fate have to play tricks on her today? She wished she could just disappear into the closing elevator doors, escaping this new nightmare.

"Good catch," the deliveryman praised, breaking the tension as he took the bags from her hands.

"No harm done," the deliveryman replied with a slight smirk, clearly amused by the encounter.

"Yeah, okay," Bethany stammered, feeling like she was just digging herself into a deeper hole. She quickly turned away, eager to find Shannon and escape the awkwardness.

It seemed like nothing could go right these days. It was almost as if fate had decided to punk her as a new hobby. Maybe this was going to be her new normal. She certainly hoped not. If that were going to be the case, she would probably become the crazy cat-lady recluse who lived alone in a hotel room.

Finally spotting Shannon's desk, Bethany let out a sigh of relief. Her bestie's welcoming smile immediately put her nerves at ease. "I sure hope you're almost ready to leave," Bethany said, grateful for the distraction.

"Yep, the man you ran into is the one I'm expecting," Shannon confirmed.

"Of course," Bethany groaned, leaning against the desk as she watched the deliveryman approach.

Shannon took the delivery and announced, "I'll be right back," before leading the deliveryman down the hall to the conference room.

Left alone for a moment, Bethany closed her eyes and took a deep breath. "Great, now I've managed to run into my childhood nemesis. Can this day get any better?" she muttered to herself with a hint of sarcasm.

But despite the awkwardness, she couldn't help but chuckle at the absurdity of the situation. "Well, at least this day can't be called boring," she thought, trying to find some humor in the chaos.

As she waited for Shannon to return, Bethany couldn't help but think that maybe a vacation or a new hobby was just what she needed to shake off these terrible memories. Who knows? Maybe running into Reggie was a sign that it was time to add some unexpected excitement to her life.

After all, if life was going to keep throwing surprises at her, she might as well learn to embrace them with a sense of humor and a dash of sass.

CHAPTER 2
REGGIE

His head was clearly not in the game. Not only had he misquoted some pretty key details, but he had also lost his place in his prepared speech at least three times. Fortunately, Adam had finally come to his rescue by standing up.

"I think it's time for us to partake of the refreshments Shannon arranged for us," Reggie announced as Adam came to walk beside him as he promptly left the front of the room.

"What's wrong with you? I've never seen you this flustered," Adam whispered loudly.

"I just keep thinking I saw someone I knew from my past. She was standing outside the conference room just after I began talking. I doubt it was her, but I guess it could've been."

"Dude, what happened to your adage of never mixing business with pleasure?"

Reggie's eyebrows drew low over his eyes until he realized Adam was just teasing him. "That's my father's quote, never mine!"

"Too right. Hey, speaking of business and pleasure, is the party still scheduled for this weekend?" Adam stopped just short of winking at him conspiratorially.

"Yep, everything's ironed out. The special guests will be staying at the best hotel in town, and we'll have a car pick them up to bring them to the party promptly at 8 pm."

"When do the girls arrive? I'd hate to miss their entrance."

"I thought you had a girlfriend, man!"

"That doesn't stop me from looking."

"So does that mean you'll be bringing this mystery girl to the party as your plus one?"

"I haven't decided yet. We're not that serious. I might just want to let loose a little and have fun."

"Oh, so she's a high-maintenance girl?"

"Aren't they all?" Adam shook his head as he stopped in front of the selection of bagels.

Reggie had his share of women, but he always enjoyed them. It did not seem like Adam appreciated the fairer sex as he should. Deciding to let it go, Reggie moved over to the donuts and selected an apple fritter.

Taking a bite of the soft, moist pastry, he could not help but think the smell of apples reminded him of Bethany in the fifth grade.

What? Where did that come from? he asked himself in dismay. *Since when do I have smell associations with her? Since apple was her favorite lip gloss when I kissed her behind the monkey bars on the playground*, he reminded himself snidely.

Suddenly feeling the need to be alone, Reggie excused himself and left the conference room. Even without conscious thought, he scanned the office waiting area for any signs of Bethany. He knew it was ridiculous. After all, he had seen her get into the elevator with Shannon. Still, he could not help wishing she would return.

Maybe, if he could talk with her, he could get the notion out of his head that he might want to get to know her again. Popping the last bite of the fritter in his mouth, he entered his office and kicked the door shut behind him. He would check his email before returning to the meeting. Surely, that would give him ample distraction from his current line of thinking.

Sitting at his desk, he entered his password into the computer and toggled over to his email server. The first few emails contained boring details about the performance of various sites, nothing new or alarming on that front. Then he came to one that stopped him dead in his tracks.

"What in the world?" he murmured as he read the details. Picking up the phone, he immediately dialed the number listed on the message.

"Highline Suites. How can I direct your call?" a woman's pleasant voice answered.

Not feeling very charitable or patient, he curtly spoke, "Connect me with the reservations manager."

"Certainly. One moment, please."

The line began playing jazz music which instantly set his nerves on edge. The shrill tones only seemed to aggravate him further as he seemed to wait an eternity for the line to connect with the manager.

"Reservations desk. Sinclair speaking."

"Sinclair, this is Reginald Bartholomew. I just received a disturbing email saying that your penthouse suites will not be available for this coming weekend. I arranged for them almost three months ago."

"I'm sorry, Mr. Bartholomew. As the email stated, we've discovered a plumbing problem that has made all of those suites as well as those below them unusable. I'm sure we can find alternate accommodations for your guests."

"I don't want them crammed in some crappy little hotel room. I needed the best for them."

"I'm sorry, sir. We'll call around and see what we can do for you. Your satisfaction is our number one priority."

"It sounds like your priority should have been maintaining your plumbing. I expect to hear back from you before the end of the day. Do you have my cell number?"

"Yes, certainly, sir."

Reggie's patience had completely evaporated by this time. He all but slammed the receiver down in his anger at the hotel's incompetence. It seemed as though his perfect plan to woo his clients was slowly unraveling. Hopefully, this would be the only setback.

Returning his attention to his emails, he barely even registered the subject lines as he clicked from one to the next. Suddenly, his eyes caught on a familiar name buried in the body of the email he had opened. Slowing down, he returned to the subject line and read, 'Auction Committee Chair Selection."

"Now what?" he breathed out in frustration. His dismay only increased as he continued reading. 'By popular vote, the committee has unanimously voted co-chairs for our annual charity auction. Congratulations to Reginald Bartholomew and Bethany Miller, who will be working together to make the event the most profitable one ever. And to that end, we'll be hosting this year's auction in beautiful New York City.'

Slamming his fists down on either side of his keyboard, he carefully re-read the email. This had to be some sort of joke. Only fate could have planned this so perfectly awful. How coincidental was it that Bethany had come up in his day three times now? He had not thought about her since graduating high school, where he had to watch her parade around in her skimpy cheerleading outfit on every game day.

Even though she always seemed to turn a blind eye to him, she had been hard to ignore. After all, he had been good friends with Pete. He'd been his football captain, after all.

Shaking his head, he wondered if there were any way to get out of his duties with the auction. And since when did Bethany have any involvement in the charity? He had never seen her at any of the meetings before. Surely, he would have noticed had she been there.

The sound of Adam clearing his throat at the office door brought Reggie's attention away from his computer screen. No amount of staring at it was going to make anything different. "What's up, Adam?"

"We're ready to get back to the meeting. Are you coming?" Adam raised his eyebrows in question.

"You know what? I think you've got this. I just received some distressing news, and I'm going to have to handle it right away."

"Anything I can help with?"

"Nope. It's not work-related, not directly anyway. Just make sure the teams know what we expect of them for this new deal. We don't want to have anyone leaving without a very clear picture of what needs to get done. I don't have to tell you how important this deal will be for the future of our company." Reggie shut down his computer and stood up. Grabbing his suit jacket from his coat rack, he strode across his office and met Adam at the door. "I'll see you tomorrow."

"Oh, okay, then," Adam stammered, clearly surprised at Reggie's sudden change of plans.

Reggie grinned at Adam's reaction, liking the idea of putting him on the spot to make sure he could handle the pressure. If everything went as he planned, Adam would take over the day-to-day operations to free Reggie up for pursuing some of his old hobbies. While he wanted to make his parents proud with his handling of the family business, he did not have the same passion for the oil industry as his father or his grandfather did.

Furthermore, he had not been brought up around the business. Rather, he had been shipped off to overseas boarding schools as soon as he was old enough. According to his mother, seven was plenty old for traveling alone. Until he got in trouble. Then it was private schools in Texas from fifth grade on.

For the most part, Reggie had not minded the separation. Even when he was home, both of his parents were too busy with their social and work calendars to have much time to devote to him. He had a better relationship with the family's staff than he ever had with his own birth parents.

Adam walked beside him as he went to catch the elevator. As soon as the doors opened, Reggie stepped inside and called out, "Good luck!" The doors silently glided shut, leaving Reggie to chuckle at Adam's look of confusion.

As soon as he got outside the building, Reggie decided against taking a drive. The fresh air and sunshine would do more for his spirit, while the exercise would get his blood pumping and help him work off some of his excess energy.

Just when he thought he might be ready to return to the office, his cell phone rang. Digging into his pocket, he managed to pick up the call before it went to voicemail. As soon as he heard the news, he knew he would have to take another lap around a larger block before he could release his anger.

According to the hotel manager, *Sinclair*, the only place with suitable accommodations at this late date was at none other than Hickory Hills Resort and Spa. Reggie stood completely still, his mind trying to understand how the hotel owned by Bethany's family would be the one place to have an opening. The longstanding feud between their families did nothing to dilute his thoughts on the kind of place Bethany's family ran.

Hanging up on the man, Reggie's fingers tightened onto his phone, threatening to break it if he were not careful. He looked around, fully expecting a camera crew to jump out of the bushes. This had to be the worst prank ever. Yet, it seemed this was the nightmare he was now living.

BETHANY

Sitting across from Shannon at the café table, Bethany felt better having company. They had spent the first twenty minutes discussing the sordid details of Pete's betrayal.

Showing her true friendship, Shannon had vowed to never speak with Alicia again after betraying Bethany so terribly.

Bethany knew this vow would be hard to keep since all of the girls ran in the same circles. Invariably, they would see one another at the spa at the very least. Also, she knew she would have to consider heading back to her house rather than staying in the hotel room her parents had so kindly offered for her while Pete gathered his personal belongings from the house.

Already, she missed her pet chickens. The little birds had been a point of contention between her and Pete anyway. There was no reason for them to suffer just because Pete was a complete scoundrel. "I've decided to head back home after lunch."

"Had enough of the spa life already?" Shannon teased, holding her coffee cup under her lip, inhaling the nutty scent of the medium roast.

"More like I'm ready to get some privacy again. I've never seen such nosy staff in all my life."

"They're just concerned. Don't give them too hard of a time."

Rolling her head to the side to release some of the tension across her shoulders, she sighed. "I know. They're all like family. A really big, nosy family. But I'm glad I've got people who care."

"Something I think Pete's finding in short supply these days."

"Good. He deserves to be alone and miserable after what he did. Can you believe it? I mean—the night before our wedding! What could have possibly been going through his mind?"

"I don't think he was using his mind."

"True. Anyway, I can't talk about him anymore. What do you have going on at work? It seemed like something big was being announced."

"Yep. Reggie's announcing the latest rollout for the newest acquisition. If everything goes right, the net worth of the company will be doubled with just this one deal."

"Oh, that's pretty impressive. Oh, hold on; my phone's ringing." Digging the phone out of her purse, she looked at the display. "I don't recognize the number."

"Are you going to answer it?"

"I guess." She hit the answer button and held the phone to her ear. After several seconds, she received the same news about being elected as co-chair for the upcoming charity auction. "Thanks for the call," she said as she ended the call.

Shifting her gaze to look over at Shannon, she said, "That's weird. I just found out I'm going to be running a charity auction in New York City."

"Oh, that's exciting! Just think of all the shopping you can do while you're there!"

"I doubt I'll have much time for that. I don't really know the city that well, and I'm going to be pretty busy keeping all the other details straight."

"Surely, they don't expect you to run the whole thing by yourself. I'm sure you'll have staff who can handle the details."

"That's the other crazy thing. Guess who's going to be my co-chair?"

Shannon pursed her lips as she tipped her head to the side, considering the options. "This is for the Batten research foundation, right?"

"Yes. When approached us, we just knew this was the cause we would back this year. Why? Do you think I'm involved in so many charities?"

"Well, you never know. Besides, you only just joined this one. I'm surprised they'd throw you into the fire so swiftly. Anyway, I give up. I can't imagine who they'd pair you with."

"None other than Reggie Bartholomew."

Eyes widening in surprise, Shannon almost choked on the sip of coffee she had just taken. Grabbing up her napkin in one hand while she abruptly set the cup down on the table with the other, she dabbed at her mouth as she got control of herself again. "What? Reggie doesn't have time for that. There's no way he's going to agree to this."

"Or else, he'll just let me do all the work myself. I wouldn't put it past him."

As if her words had caused him to materialize, Reggie walked around the corner of the block. From the expression on his face, something had gone wrong. Looking back to Shannon, Bethany asked, "I thought Reggie was stuck at work on that big deal. Why do you suppose he looks like he's ready to hit someone?"

"What? Are you sure?" Shannon asked, turning in her chair to see Reggie swiftly approaching them.

Bethany could not help but stare at him. Even angry, he had a confidence about him that almost made her salivate. She wished she could find a man who was so passionate about life. Pete sure had proved to be a huge disappointment.

Reggie's eyes locked onto Bethany's. Without any warning, he took the last several steps to close the distance between them before coming to an abrupt stop directly in front of her.

"Just what do you think you're doing? Why are you suddenly all over my life? And more to the point, who did you pay off?"

CHAPTER 3

BETHANY

Sitting in utter disbelief, Bethany stared up at Reggie, not knowing what the man could possibly be talking about. After a few seconds, her own anger stirred as the meaning of his words finally registered in her head.

She fumed at the idea of him accusing her of paying someone off. Standing up, she moved forward until she came within inches of his face where she could feel the heat of his rage radiating off of him in waves.

With a measured tone of barely controlled anger, she spat out, "What in the world are you talking about? How have I done anything to you? If not for this afternoon's mishap in your office hallway, I haven't even thought about you since the fifth grade!"

"Hah! Likely story. Explain to me how you managed to weasel your way into the charity auction then?"

"Is that what this is about? I didn't do anything of the kind. I only just found out about that appointment a few minutes ago." She looked down at Shannon as if for her agreement.

"It's true, Reggie," Shannon corroborated. "I was here when she got the phone call."

Reggie looked daggers down at Shannon for a split second before shifting his gaze back to Bethany's fiery eyes. "Then explain to me why you were at my office? Were you spying on my business?"

A bark of incredulous outrage erupted from her lips before she could stop it. This man knew no bounds. She was going to have to reconsider his success if he thought about other people in such a manner.

Deciding to take a calm approach to his obvious lack of common sense, she breathed deeply through her nose to center herself. Instead of receiving clarity, she inhaled Reggie's masculine scent, sparking something familiar and alarming inside of her. To mask her confusion, she spoke quietly, "Look, Reggie; I don't know what's gotten into you, but I suggest you take a chill pill. I came over to take Shannon out to lunch. No conspiracy theories, no agenda other than to get out of the hotel for a few minutes."

Seeing his demeanor soften slightly, Bethany thought the encounter was ready to be over. She would like to get back to her quiet lunch with her friend. There had been enough drama in her life as of late. Unfortunately, Reggie's next statement disabused her of that notion.

"Yeah, about your hotel. How'd you manage to get—? Oh, never mind. I can see I won't be getting any straight answers out of you." With that cryptic remark spoken, Reggie made a cutting gesture with his hand before he turned and stormed away from them.

With raised eyebrows, Bethany sank into her chair again. "What was that all about?" She glanced around them to see the interested stares of the other patrons. Even without trying, she had managed to make a spectacle of herself yet again.

Maybe she should have stayed alone in her hotel room after all. She certainly did not need to have any other scandals reported about her in the newspaper. One was bad enough.

"I have no idea, but that certainly wasn't Reggie's usual behavior. Are you okay?"

"I'm fine." Quirking one eyebrow, she added, "I'm used to people staring at me."

"Nobody's staring," Shannon replied swiftly, her gaze shifting to those around them. "Okay, maybe a few people were staring, but they all saw how Reggie acted. You didn't do anything other than stay calm. It was pretty impressive, actually."

"Yeah, that's me. Resilient and cold. Do you know, that's how Pete described me when I confronted him about his indiscretion?"

"He's a complete jerk, Bethany. Don't put any store in anything he said to you. You deserve so much better than him. I'm sure you'll find someone who can treat you like the queen you are."

"I think it'll be a while before I start looking. I just need some time to be me. For my entire adult life, I've been dating Pete. It's high time I started learning who I am by myself. I don't need a man to make me happy."

"That's the spirit. Besides, you've got your chickens!"

A burst of laughter left her lips as she nodded her agreement. "That's right. Those chickens need me! Wow. That sounds even more pathetic than adopting a dozen cats and becoming a recluse."

"I thought you were allergic to cats."

The waiter chose that moment to drop off the receipt for the bill. "Thanks for coming out with me today, Shannon. You really helped."

"Anytime, babe."

"Alright, let's get you back to the office. It sounds like you might be needed more there."

"I was just thinking the same thing. It's a good thing you had me eat. I think I'm going to be busy with damage control."

"Yeah, maybe you can look into getting Reggie a new personality. That'd be the first thing I'd do."

"He's not usually like that, Bethany. Honest." Shannon reached out and touched the back of Bethany's hand.

For some reason, the soft touch broke through her foul mood. Completely unbidden, tears sprang into her eyes. "I know, Shannon." Wiping the tears away before they could ruin her makeup, she said, "I don't know why I'm crying. It's not like I did or said anything to deserve Reggie's tirade."

"No, you didn't. Unfortunately, we were in the wrong place at the right time. C'mon. Let's head back."

Bethany nodded, picking up her purse from the ground where she had left it. Even angry at her, Reggie still managed to stir up her old feelings for him. How was she going to work with him for the charity auction if all they did was fight with one another? This was going to prove very taxing. Hopefully, she would be up for it.

REGGIE

"What was I thinking going off on her like that?" Reggie muttered to himself. He thought his day could not get any worse, but he had managed to take it to a new level of awful. Feeling doubly stupid for venting his anger at Bethany, he strode down the street. If only he had kept his mouth shut. It was inexcusable to take out his frustration in such a childish, public manner.

"I can't just leave things like this," he muttered. Now he was going to have to apologize to her. Hopefully, she would come back to the office, so he could do so. "That's stupid," he chided himself immediately. That seemed like too easy of an out for him.

"No, I'm going to have to do something more." A realization struck him in that instant. "Now, I'm going to have to accept that nomination to the charity auction, if only to take the burden of the task away from her." Reggie disregarded the people staring at him as he spoke aloud to himself. He did not worry about their opinion of him; he just wanted to make things right with Bethany.

As soon as he made up his mind about a solution to his latest problem, he felt a sense of rightness overtake him. He would apologize to her, but he would also prove his sincerity with his actions.

Not only would he accept the nomination, but he would also devote every waking moment to make sure the auction was a complete success. To this end, he planned on officially appointing Adam as lead to the acquisition project. He had been pushing him to more responsibility, and this was going to become his ultimate test.

Each step toward the office solidified his new resolve. He could feel the burdens of responsibility begin to fall away from him. While the business was important for his future, he did not feel the same level of commitment to the job itself. Sure, he loved spending the money from the profits, but he hated being chained to the office.

He would make his excuse of the auction to allow him to get away for more than just a few hours in the evening. His mind reeled over what he could do to fill his newfound time. "After the auction, of course," he reminded himself. A smile formed on his lips as he thought about how confused Bethany would be with his change of heart.

No longer did he feel frustrated or confused about the interactions he had found himself in with Bethany. Rather than attempting to avoid her, he decided he would embrace every opportunity where she came into contact with him.

If fate wanted to punk him, he would certainly find a way to take advantage of it. No longer would he be the victim of fate's persnickety ways. He was going to take charge of his future. Even if that meant Bethany would be a part of it.

His strides lengthened, and he felt a smile tugging the corners of his mouth upward. Yes, this was going to be a great day of change. Rounding the corner, he spotted a cute little sports car pulling up to the front of his building. Raising his eyebrows in appreciation of the fine car, he planned to find out who owned it.

When he spotted Shannon getting out of the passenger side, he frowned slightly. Coming to a stop beside the vehicle, he leaned forward and peered into the vehicle. The smile widened on his face as he saw Bethany staring suspiciously at him from behind the steering wheel, which she clutched tightly.

"Nice car, Bethany." He could see her eyes widen with surprise. To keep her from replying with a smart comment, he swiftly added, "I'm sorry for how I spoke to you back there. It was completely inexcusable. I'd like to make it up to you somehow."

"Okay," Bethany drawled slowly, her head tipping to the side as she considered Reggie carefully.

Seeing as how she did not shut him down immediately, Reggie decided to press his advantage of surprise by asking, "How about dinner tonight?" He loved how her eyes widened with surprise. Why had it taken him so long to notice how stunning she actually looked?

CHAPTER 4
BETHANY

Her mind raced with how to answer his invitation. Not forgetting his cutting remarks all through school and followed recently with his humiliating display not more than twenty minutes ago, she decided to pass. "I'm busy," she stated, her hands clenching the steering wheel as if it were her only hold on reality.

"Great!" Reggie began but then blustered for a second as he realized she had turned him down. "What? Why not?" He leaned his forearms against the window sill as he tried to entice her to change her mind.

"Um, I don't think that needs an explanation." She tipped her head back toward the restaurant she had just left. "That display back there only proved you haven't changed a bit since high school."

"I just apologized for that! Can't you give a guy a second chance?"

"Normally, I would. But you've proved yourself unworthy of my time. Good day, Reginald." Not wanting to give him another opportunity to convince her to go out with him, she revved her engine a little before waiting for an opening in the traffic. As soon as she had her chance, she pulled away from the curb.

Even though she tried to resist the urge, she looked in her rearview mirror. She could see Reggie standing on the sidewalk, staring after her. His dejected expression instantly made her feel guilty. Maybe she should have gone out with him.

"What? What am I thinking? I don't want anything to do with Reggie. He's the last man on Earth who I'd want to voluntarily spend an evening with!" Even saying the words out loud felt forced and untrue.

She had never gotten over her fifth-grade crush on him. If only her friends had not made such a fuss about the kiss, then maybe something could have happened with the two of them. If only—if only. That seemed to be the mantra of her life.

If only Pete had not turned out to be a lying, cheating bastard, then she would be happily married right now. "No, I'm better off making a go of being alone for a while," she announced to herself. Even as the words fell from her lips, she felt loneliness begin to descend onto her shoulders.

The burden felt too heavy to bear. It was time to go home. Time to face the home she would have shared with Pete. After all, she loved the property. She had loved it from the moment she had seen the picture of the white picket fence on the real estate website. Luckily, she had purchased the house on her own. Otherwise, she would have had to sell it to buy out Pete's half.

Just thinking about returning home brought her some measure of closure. Besides, she needed to check on her chickens. They were always a source of pleasure for her. She smiled just thinking about their silly antics every time she tossed bits of grain out for them.

By the time she pulled into the hotel parking lot, she knew she was checking out of her room for good. No longer would she have to endure the endless questions and looks of pity from the employees. Well-meaning or not, she was ready for some privacy again.

She managed to make it to her room without too much fuss, which in and of itself was a minor miracle. With her bag packed and in hand, she thought she might be able to get away from everyone without anyone trying to convince her to change her mind. Just as she opened the door for the last time, she came face-to-face with her mother.

The smile died on her mother's lips as she took notice of the packed bag. "Are you going somewhere?"

"Yes, Mom. I'm going home."

"No, my dear. You shouldn't be alone at a time like this. Here, let me help you unpack." Rachael reached for Bethany's bag.

Seeing what was going to happen, Bethany instantly turned to keep her bag away from her mother. "No, Mom. I need to have some privacy. Besides, my chickens need me. It's about time I started putting my life back together." That sounded pathetic, even to her own ears. An inspiration struck, and she added, "Besides, I've got plans for tonight."

"Right. Plans with your chickens, right?" Rachael's eyes narrowed suspiciously. She could see right through her daughter's lame explanation.

"No, Mom. I'm going on a dinner date. I'm sorry, Mom, but I've got to be going if I don't want to be late." She tried to step outside of her room, but her mother was not giving an inch.

"You can't just drop a bomb on me like that without giving me more details. Who're you going out with? Don't you think it's a bit early to be seeing anyone else? He'd just be a rebound anyway, and those relationships don't ever work out."

"Geez, Mom. Give me some credit. It's not a romantic dinner date. I'm going to dinner with the co-chair of the charity auction. We've got lots of details to work out."

"Oh? Do tell. What's his name? Do I know him?" Rachael reached out and grabbed her daughter's elbow as she steered her out of the room and toward the elevator. "Maybe something will spark between the two of you." Seeing Bethany's look of scorn, she added, "You never know."

"I know, Mom. The co-chair is none other than Reggie Bartholomew." Seeing her mother's nose wrinkle with disgust, she knew she had struck the right chord. "Now, no more matchmaking, Mom. I've got to keep myself busy, and this is a good start." Bethany punched the elevator button and had the satisfaction of seeing her mother try to come up with something positive to say about her evening's plans.

"I'm sure you'll do amazing with the auction. You're a natural-born planner."

The elevator doors opened, and Bethany almost sighed with relief. Giving her mother a quick peck on the cheek, she stepped into the lift before the doors slid shut. "I love you, Mom." Her relief was short-lived as she realized she would have to eat crow when she called Reggie to accept his invitation. She blew a frustrated breath out of her lips as she tried to reconcile her decision with her heart.

She really could just consider this a business dinner. Then it would not really be anything scandalous. Would Reggie see it the same way? "I'm just going to have to make it crystal clear to him what my intentions are for the evening. If he wants to prove to me that he's changed, then this'll be a good test."

The elevator doors slid open at the first-floor lobby. Crowds of people were standing in groups scattered throughout the expansive space. She knew of this weekend's convention and was doubly happy to be removing herself from the chaos which would certainly be present with this many people milling about.

With a wave at the desk clerk, she made her way to the revolving doors. The doorman nodded to her and noticed the bag slung over her shoulder. "Are you checking out?"

"Yes, Chris. It's time I went home. Can you let Pricilla know? She seemed a bit busy at the moment for me to bother."

"Sure thing, Beth. I'm going to miss seeing you around."

"Thanks, Chris. You've always been the bright spot in my days as well. My chickens need me, though."

Chris laughed as he gestured for her to go through the revolving door. "Have a nice evening."

Bethany took the opening to leave and stepped into the doorway. Even as she made her way through, she noticed a nicely dressed man on the opposite side. As her eyes traveled up his muscular body, her appreciation for his form filled her senses. That is until she noticed the face attached to the body. Reggie. What was he doing here?

He seemed to see her at the same time. She hurried away from the door and toward her car. Maybe she could get to her car before he could decide to chase her down.

"Bethany!" he called out.

Her steps faltered. She was going to have to talk to him or make a scene in the parking lot.

Besides, why am I trying to run from him? I wanted to talk to him anyway, right? Yeah, that's what I'm telling myself. Coming to a stop, she turned and waited for him to catch up with her.

"What're you doing here?" she rudely asked. She hated sounding snarky, but he just brought out the worst in her. It was an old habit, one he had done his best to instill in her.

"I wanted to see if I could change your mind about dinner. I really am sorry about everything."

"Everything?" She cocked her head to the side as her eyebrows rose. "Are you sure you want to go there?"

"Yes. Bethany, don't you think we've taken this animosity far enough. I mean, we're not kids anymore. Can't we just agree to let the past remain in the past? I mean, after all, we're going to be working together for the auction. It'll be a lot more fun if we're not at each other's throats all the time."

"Oh, so it's for the sake of the auction then? Nothing else?"

"Can't we start there?" Reggie's hand reached out toward her as if he wanted to touch her, but he stopped short.

Bethany stared at his hand, her mind instantly wondering what it would feel like to have him touch her. Would she feel the electrical spark she imagined feeling back in the fifth grade? What? She wasn't a ten-year-old anymore.

She inhaled through her nose as she tried to come up with a non-snarky answer. That was a mistake. She could smell his masculine scent again. It intoxicated her senses immediately. She had to look away and compose herself.

"Fine. But it's just going to be a business dinner. Don't get any other ideas. I still don't like you much, but we do have to work out the details for the auction."

"Really? Great! Okay, why don't you meet me at my house at six?"

"Wait! Why your house? I thought we'd just go to a restaurant or something." She immediately regretted accepting his invitation. This was starting to feel too personal, too soon.

"Easy, girl. I've got one of the best chefs in the nation at my disposal. Besides, I don't want to have to talk over the noise of other patrons while we're working. Trust me; I won't try to make any moves on you. You're safe on that score." He looked her up and down, his eyes seeming scornful of her appearance.

Feeling twitchy at his comment, she huffed before she said, "Fine. Have Shannon send me your address. She's got my cell number."

"Great! See you later then." Reggie rocked forward on his toes, his excitement at her acceptance obvious in his demeanor.

Bethany nodded curtly, feeling foolish even as she did it. Rather than try to explain herself any further, she turned on her heels and resumed walking toward her car. Even without looking back, she could feel Reggie's piercing stare watching her every move. Her hips began to sway more than usual, and she instantly wondered what had gotten into her.

She stifled a groan of dismay at herself as she pushed the button on her remote to open her trunk. Throwing her bag into the small space, she rushed to get into the car, just to get away from any further embarrassment. As she suspected, Reggie stood rooted to the spot where she had left him. He waved with a foolish grin on his face as she drove past him.

He really was too much. How could she possibly stay mad at him if he kept acting so silly?

Easily, she reminded herself. *Think of all the times he publicly scorned me in the halls in high school. Oh, and remember the time he warned Pete about kissing me? Yeah, that was mortifying, to say the least.*

But that was in the past. Maybe it was time to let that go and see what the future held in store for her. Could she do that? How could she not? Her life was already blown to bits by Pete's betrayal.

How much worse could it get?

"I've got to stop saying things like that," Bethany groaned to herself. "I don't want to tempt fate any more than I already have. The next thing you know, she'll be arranging for Reggie and me to get together."

Would that be so terrible? she asked herself. *Yes! There are so many other men out there. I don't need to get myself attached to the one person who tormented me for so many years. Nope. Not going to happen. Not in this lifetime.*

Bethany's drive home was a blur. All she could think about was how good Reggie looked in his suit. She loved how he smelled; it made her heart race just remembering it. "Stop it!" she cried out in dismay.

She pulled into the driveway, sighing with relief that Pete's car was nowhere in sight. Fate had not decided to have him be the icing on the cake today after all. She glanced at the clock, realizing she would have plenty of time to check on the chickens and relax in a luxurious bubble bath before she even had to think about getting ready for her date.

"It's not a date!" she instantly corrected herself. She grabbed her bag out of the trunk and dumped it on the front porch as she stalked her way through the yard toward the pen where the chickens lived. The happy sounds of their clucking prompted her to walk faster.

Grabbing up the bucket of grain, she smiled at how they began running toward her. At least something was happy to see her home again. Well, they were happy to get the treats.

Oh well. It makes me happy to see them enjoy the food.

Her bath would have to wait a bit longer. She needed to soak in the joyful vibes from her feathered friends.

CHAPTER 5

REGGIE

The euphoria refused to leave Reggie as he stood in the parking lot. She agreed to have dinner with him. Tonight. He would have her in his house before the night was through.

Instantly, he realized he was going to have to make some serious plans. Whipping out his phone, he called home and let his chef know about the change in plans. As expected, Jeff's voice sounded both excited and irritated by the short notice. He knew Jeff was up for the challenge of only having five hours to create a masterpiece.

Next, he had to get back to work and have Shannon put together some plans for him as well. He needed flowers delivered and his dry cleaning picked up. Not to mention, Shannon needed to send his home address to Bethany.

Maybe he could get Bethany's phone number out of Shannon as well. He decided not to push his luck. He wanted

Bethany to give him her number personally. It had to be her idea.

With his thoughts racing, Reggie returned to his car. Earlier today, he never would have imagined being this excited to have Bethany come over to his house for dinner. Heck, he never even considered speaking to her; now he was planning a date. Well, not a date exactly.

This was more like two business associates getting together to plan an event. That thought brought him right back down to Earth. He hated mixing business with pleasure. The lavish parties he threw were a testament to that fact. If he had to have business dealings, he sure as heck was going to make everyone forget anything about business.

Driving back to the office was just a blur. He wondered what type of meal Jeff would have for them. Should he dress up or just keep things casual? Would Bethany arrive in jeans, or would she wear a dress to show off her stunning figure? He hoped the latter.

The guard in the lobby nodded politely to him as he passed. Normally, Reggie would not have given him any notice, but today he smiled and said, "Great day, huh?"

The puzzled look on the guard's face made Reggie smile even broader. As soon as he stepped in front of the elevator, the doors opened as if they had been waiting just for him. He stepped aside to allow several people to exit the lift before he entered the now-empty space.

It was amazing how his whole perspective on life had changed only in a matter of hours. Could it be possible that he and Bethany were destined to be together? What did fate have in store for him?

The lift jolted as it came to a stop on the sixteenth floor. Instantly, Reggie wondered if that were fate telling him not to get ahead of himself. After all, Bethany had been the source of all of his problems for over fifteen years. He would be wise to carefully tread until he knew for sure what her intentions were with him.

When he stopped in front of Shannon's desk, he had to impatiently wait for her to get rid of whoever was on the phone. From the sounds of it, it was someone he had been attempting to arrange a meeting with for the last two months. He hoped this was the case; he needed to meet with Andrew to go over some of the details of the land purchase he needed to button up before this huge deal could be brought to fruition.

Shannon smiled up at him as she hung up the phone. "Good news. Andrew has time to meet with you tonight. I arranged for six o'clock drinks at the Irish Pub."

"Tonight? Ugh!" Reggie drummed his fingers on the surface of the desk. "Okay, I think I can make this work."

"Why? What's going on?"

Seeing her disappointment, he said, "Bethany agreed to have dinner at my house tonight. I don't want to cancel."

Shannon's eyebrows rose almost to her hairline in her surprise. "I see. I thought she turned you down."

"What can I say? I'm persuasive when I need to be. Besides, we need to iron out the details of the charity auction."

"Right," Shannon slowly said as she looked away, hardly even attempting to hide her grin at his not-so-subtle arrogance. "So, what do you need me to do?"

"First, call Bethany and convince her to move dinner to seven. Then call Jeff and let him know he'll get an extra hour to make dinner." Reggie crossed his arms, his fingertips tapping against his bicep as he tried to recall the other details he had wanted.

Snapping his fingers as he remembered, he said, "Call the florist and have them deliver several bouquets for the dining table, foyer, and the living room. I want the place to smell amazing. Do you know what her favorite flower is?" Not stopping to see if she did or not, he continued, "Then text her my home address."

Shannon scribbled her notes furiously as he kept talking.

Just as Reggie entered his office, he turned abruptly, holding onto the doorframe as he leaned out to say, "And have my dry cleaning delivered to my house. I doubt I'll have time to change, but I'd like the opportunity to do so if I can."

"On it," Shannon called out to him as the door clicked shut.

Reggie strode across his office. His mind was anywhere other than the problems here at work. Thank goodness he had Adam taking charge of the new deal. He would have to give him a promotion and a raise if he managed to pull everything off as they planned. It would totally be worth it to have Adam in charge.

His father had been too consumed with the day-to-day operations. Everything else came second to the job, including his family. Reggie wanted something different for himself. Although the money the business provided for him was obscene, he wondered if it were actually worth it.

Thinking of what his money could do for him, he picked up his phone and tapped the intercom. "Shannon, order a car to pick up Bethany. It wouldn't do for her to get lost. Besides, it'd be harder for her to back out if she knows someone is on his way to get her."

"True. Sounds good, boss."

Without another thought, Reggie disconnected the call with Shannon. Yes, money could bring him so much joy. Maybe he should plan an extravagant getaway for himself and Bethany. He could tell her that he just wanted to have some quiet time to plan the auction.

Where could they go? He liked that little village in Bora Bora. They could take the private jet, and he could impress her with that as well.

What was he thinking? Why was he trying to go out of his way to impress her? Only this morning, he was comparing her to a black widow spider. Could she possibly have ensnared him so swiftly? Was he deluding himself? Maybe.

No, he would slow things down. Dinner tonight would be her first test. If she managed to not make any digs at him, he might consider what they could do for their second date. "It's not a date," he mumbled, still trying to convince himself of that fact. Somehow, his subconscious merely chuckled at his delusion. It was definitely a date, one a long-time coming.

BETHANY

Her toe had only touched the hot water of her bubble bath when the phone rang. Sighing with exasperation, she pulled her leg away from the tub and turned instead to head back into her bedroom to grab the phone. Picking up the receiver, she wondered who knew she would be home. It was not like she had been there more than two hours.

"Hey, Beth, it's me, Shannon."

"Hey! I was wondering who would know to call me here. What's up?" Bethany tried to play ignorant. She was actually surprised it had taken Shannon this long to call her. Surely, the girl would be wondering why she had accepted Reggie's invitation.

"I made a mistake, and now I need to fix it."

"What's going on?" Bethany swiftly sat on the edge of her bed, wondering what Shannon could possibly have done wrong.

"Before Reggie told me about your dinner plans, I arranged for him to have drinks with a client he's been trying to see for the past two months. You're not going to believe when he was available."

"Let me guess. Six o'clock tonight?"

"You got it. I'm sorry, Beth."

Instantly relieved to get out of the dinner, she sighed and said, "That's okay. I was merely using him as an excuse to get away from my mother at the hotel. You've actually done me a huge favor."

"Well, about that—Reggie wants you to meet him at his house at seven instead. He's sending a car to pick you up."

"Ugh," Beth replied.

"Please say you'll go. Reggie'll make my life so difficult if you cancel on him because of me."

Closing her eyes, she pinched the bridge of her nose as she wished there was some way out of this. "Fine. Tell him I'll be there."

"Oh, Beth, thank you! I must say, I could hardly believe he had managed to get you to agree to meet with him. As far as I knew, you two have been arch enemies forever. I guess it makes more sense that your mother was involved in the decision."

"Why? What'd Reggie say about it?

"Something stupid, like his irresistible charm."

Bursting out laughing, Bethany could hardly believe Reggie's arrogance. "Yeah, no! I was just happy that I didn't have to eat crow and ask him to reconsider my first refusal. We'll just let him think this was a win for him."

"He'll never hear differently from me," Shannon replied, her chuckling sounding softly through the receiver.

"Well, my bath's waiting for me. Now that I have an extra hour, I might even start reading that paranormal romance book I got last week."

"Sounds perfect. Do you need me to call to wake you up in two hours?"

"You know me too well. No, I'll be fine. Thanks for the offer, though."

Bethany hung up the phone, still shaking her head at Reggie's audacity in thinking it was his charm that had caused her to agree to meet with him. If only he knew! It spoke volumes that she would rather spend the evening with someone she despised than having to spend another night under her mother's watchful eyes and spies disguised as employees.

Picking up her copy of *Falling for the Wolf Girl* from her bedside table, she wished she could find someone who wanted to be with her as much as the man on this cover appeared to want to be with the woman he held. Was it too much to ask for someone like that? Apparently, she scoffed to herself.

Returning to the bathroom, she grabbed another caramel apple bath bomb and let it slip from her fingers into the steaming water. Almost instantly, the water began to froth and turn a light shade of green. The crisp smell of apple hit her nostrils, and she immediately recalled all of the memories associated with that smell.

Funny how the mind worked. She first recalled loving the scent when her mother bought her a makeup kit science project. She had developed her own scented lip gloss using the apple oil which had come with it. Not only did it keep her from biting her nails, but she had also been wearing it the day that Reggie kissed her on the playground.

"Where did that come from?" she murmured, pausing in the act of stepping into the water. Rolling her eyes, she wished she could go back to that day and do it over. What if nobody had seen them? Would they have stayed friends throughout the years? Would he have been the one to ask her to marry him? Would he have cheated on her as Pete had?

With the dark turn of her thoughts, she shook her head. Not wanting to think about Pete, she opened the paperback book and started reading. Maybe reading about some fictional characters' lives would keep her from stewing over what might have been.

Soon she was lost in the story. The water surrounding her grew tepid, but she hardly noticed. It was not until she felt herself actively shivering as she tried to turn the page that she realized how cold the water had become. With a grunt of disgust at her inattentiveness, she realized she would have to take a warm shower to prevent hypothermia from setting in.

Okay, maybe that was an exaggeration, but she hated the idea of wasting time just getting warm again. She tossed the book onto the counter by the sink as she stood up. Pulling the plug, she waited for the water to lower before reaching for her towel.

Unfortunately, the drain chose that moment to stop working. A single burp of air came up from the drain spout, but nothing else happened. How many times had she asked Pete to take care of this?

Ugh, now she was going to have to fix the dumb thing. Looking around, she had two choices: the drain snake or the toilet plunger. Either one of them was gross, but what choice did she have? As the sole owner of the house, it was now her responsibility to handle the maintenance issues.

Not wanting to have to pick off disgusting hair and goo from the snake, she opted for the toilet plunger. After slipping several times on the wet tile floor, she made it back to the edge of the tub. Kneeling on the floor, she positioned the plunger over the drain and shoved it down as hard as she could.

Of course, the water splashed up and hit her in the face. Luckily, it narrowly missed her mouth by a millimeter, but she grimaced in disgust all the same. With the disgusting and cold water dripping down her face, she had to plunge the tool down several more times before the water decided it was able to flush swiftly down the drain.

Even though she had warmed up from the exertion, she definitely needed a shower now. There was no way she would risk getting E. coli, however remote the possibility. With lightning speed, she washed up, soaping her face at least three times just to be certain. Her skin glowed bright pink from all her scrubbing by the time she exited the shower.

Glancing at the clock, her eyes grew large to see that it was already half after six. Where had the time gone? Surely, her bath had not been that long.

Dropping her towel where she stood, she raced out of the bathroom and practically dove into her walk-in closet.

She clawed through the hanging clothes, desperate to find something suitable. Should she dress up or keep things casual? Did she want Reggie to notice what he had missed out on?

"No way!" she spoke aloud, startling herself. "This isn't a date, and I don't need to impress him." She grabbed a cashmere sweater and a pair of designer jeans and left the closet. Selecting a matching pair of panties and bra, she still could not shake the idea of wanting to impress him.

Her resolve to stay without a man in her life proved to be more complicated than she originally imagined. Of course, she had not had a sexy man asking her out to dinner when she had made the impetuous decision. "It's just for business," she mumbled, not even managing to sound convincing to her own ears.

CHAPTER 6
REGGIE

Reggie kept glancing at his watch between sips of his beer. Who knew Andrew could blather on so long about nothing? His initial idea of making this a quick get-together and then heading home to change was swiftly disabused as Andrew insisted on telling the same stories over and over again.

Of course, it probably did not help that Andrew was already three sheets to the wind even before they ordered their first drink. It made Reggie wonder if working with him was a good idea after all. However, they did not need to become friends for the deal to go through. All he needed was his signature on the contract before they could forever part ways.

When Andrew almost slipped off of the bar stool for the third time, Reggie decided to take matters into his own hands. Grabbing the older man by the elbow, he said, "I think we've had enough talking for tonight. We need to get you into a hotel for the night. I know just the place."

Steering him clear of the stool, Reggie managed to get a wad of cash from his pocket to throw onto the bar before moving them both out of the bustle of the noisy bar. Feeling the man begin to struggle out of his grip, he tightened his hold.

"But I wasn't done with my drink," Andrew slurred, glancing back over his shoulder to see if his glass was still located on the bar.

"It was only ice left, Andrew. We can finish this conversation tomorrow once you've sobered up." Reggie was not about to let the man out of his sight until he had him safely in the hands of the nearest hotel. Standing outside, he realized he was in no shape to drive either. Looking from left to right, Reggie noticed the sign for Hickory Hills Resort and Spa and decided on the spur of the moment to take Andrew there directly.

Seeing as it was only about a football field away, he thought they could manage quite handily on foot. The fresh air and exercise would help to sober himself up. With a plan in place, Reggie began hauling Andrew alongside him. He did not bother trying to engage in conversation, nor did he try to answer Andrew's many attempts to prevent him from taking him to the hotel.

Once they reached the lobby, Andrew's complaints had reached a new level of volume, enough to draw the attention of the patrons inside the lobby. Reggie wished for nothing more than to get the man registered to a room and safely tucked in a bed so he could be away from here.

Within fifteen minutes, his plan had been taken care of, and Andrew was given over to the manager, who had insisted on giving him personal service. Reggie's estimation of the hotel rose considerably. Maybe his father had been wrong about this place. It hardly seemed appropriate for the manager to be so pleasant and accommodating if they were participating in illicit acts on the side.

In any event, Reggie leaned against the counter, sighing with relief to be done with Andrew. Now, he needed to get a lift back to his house. Twisting his chin from one side to the other, he felt the tension leave his neck as both sides cracked. He turned his eyes to the woman at the desk, noting her nametag, and asked, "Can you call me a driver, Pricilla? I don't think I'm in any condition to drive right now."

"Sure thing, Mr. Bartholomew," Pricilla replied cheerfully.

Only after Reggie sat in the back seat of a private car did he realize he had never given the name to the hotel staff. The card he had charged the room to was only in his business's name. Yet the woman knew exactly who he was.

With his head resting on the back of the seat, he grinned foolishly at the idea of people recognizing him on sight. He knew it happened for his father all the time, but now it seemed people were beginning to know who he was as well.

They pulled into the driveway of his estate. Reggie hoped he had arrived before Bethany. Somehow, he doubted he would be so lucky.

BETHANY

Having the car come pick her up certainly made it harder to keep in mind that this was simply a business dinner. Certainly not a date. She had to remind herself yet again as the Lincoln Town car pulled up in front of the enormous estate, which she had to assume was Reggie's house.

She could hardly imagine finding such a huge place to be at all homey. She much preferred her three-bedroom cottage to this monstrosity. Hopefully, Reggie had the good sense to hire a designer to decorate. Otherwise, she would think the walls would be covered in dark wallpaper or paint and adorned in either weaponry or trophy heads.

As the driver parked in the circular driveway just outside the front door, she continued to gawk at the huge fountain, the six-car garage, and the massive columns holding up the porch awning. The entire presentation was over the top, just like she always thought of Reggie. All show and no substance.

Hearing the driver clear his throat pulled her out of her reverie. With a start, she managed to get out of the vehicle without making too much of a fool of herself. She clutched her purse in both hands. Should she tip the driver, or would that be considered rude?

Luckily, the driver merely smiled and shut the door as soon as she cleared out of the way. "Have a nice dinner," he announced before smartly turning and walking back to the driver's seat to drive away.

Bethany simply stared as he drove around the side of the garage. Of course, he was retained staff, nothing but the best for Reggie. She turned back toward the front door, wondering if she should knock or if she would rather get her bearings before going inside.

This whole idea began to feel wrong. She should have stayed at home where she could unpack and get herself put together more. More than ever, she wished she had driven herself so she could just get back in her car and go home. Glancing longingly toward the gated entrance, she had her back to the door.

"Won't you come inside?" a man's voice asked.

Whipping around, her eyes wide with shock, she saw a man dressed smartly in a suit waiting for her response. "Oh, yes. I'm sorry; I didn't see you there. I was admiring the estate."

"Master Reggie takes great pride in having it perfectly manicured. He's not home at present, but I'd be more than happy to get you settled with a drink."

"Yes, that'd be lovely," Bethany responded, suddenly grateful for the opportunity to take in her surroundings without having to worry about Reggie. With quick steps, she climbed the stairs and entered the house.

Much to her surprise, the interior was light and airy. Just inside the door, a massive table sat front and center in the foyer, adorned with an equally large bouquet of fresh flowers. Bethany could only imagine how much those fancy blossoms must have cost.

She followed the butler into the sitting room near the front door. Just like the foyer, this room contained fashionable furniture, more flowers, and floor-to-ceiling windows, which flooded the room with light. Running her hand along the edge of the baby grand piano, she wondered if Reggie played or if it were simply a statement piece of furniture.

"Would you like wine or a mixed drink?" the man asked.

"I'd love a glass of Moscato if you have it." Not much of a drinker, she suddenly worried if it were rude to ask for something so specific.

"A lovely choice. I have just the perfect one for you. Please have a seat and make yourself at home. I'll return shortly."

"Thank you," she murmured as she watched the butler turn on his heel and walk back the way he came. She had to give it to Reggie; his staff was very professional. Almost too professional. Were they always so aloof? If so, Reggie's home life must be lonelier than she would have imagined.

Although, hearing about his parties begged to differ with him staying lonely. Over the years, Shannon had filled her in about the crazy stunts Reggie had pulled at his infamous events. Some of the more outlandish stories made her cringe with embarrassment. No, the party life was not for her. She enjoyed the simple things.

Taking a seat where she could enjoy the view outside, she glanced down at her watch, noting it was five minutes after seven o'clock. "At least one of us is on time," she mumbled to herself. Again, a noise startled her. Shifting her glance over to the doorway, she noticed the butler returning with a single glass poised on a silver tray. So ostentatious.

When he approached her, he leaned forward at his waist and offered her the glass of wine. "Moscato for the lady," he said, his expression slightly amused.

"Thank you," Bethany replied formally, taking the long-stemmed glass between her fingers. Bringing it up to her nose, she inhaled the lovely floral scent of the wine. Knowing the butler would remain nearby until she approved of her drink, she brought the glass to her lips and took a small sip, letting the fruity liquid float over her tongue.

"Mmm. This is perfect. Thank you so much."

"My pleasure. If you require anything else, just ring this bell." He took a dainty bell from his front pocket and silently set it down onto the table in front of her.

"Okay, um, thanks." Nothing could convince her to ever ring that bell. Seeing the butler begin to retreat, she hastily asked, "Do you know how much longer Reggie will be?"

"He just called to let us know he's on his way. I expect him here within the next few minutes." He nodded curtly and left the room.

"Nothing to do but drink and wait, I guess." Bethany sat back on the couch and took a sip of her wine. The silence settled around her, much like it was in her own home. Before she knew it, the wine was gone, and still, Reggie had yet to make his appearance.

Feeling restless, she stood up to begin her first circuit of the room. Picking up various picture frames and trinkets, she occupied her time until a sound registered from outside. Turning, she noticed a Prius pulling up in front of the house.

Thinking it did not look like anything Reggie would drive, her interest piqued. Moving forward, she stood to the side of the window, peeking outside where she could see the back door being opened by the butler. That man really did not miss a beat. It seemed he was everywhere at just the right time.

Reggie stepped out of the vehicle. The smile he gave the butler certainly seemed genuine; maybe the staff was all his friends after all. Bethany wished she still had her glass of wine to hold as her nerves suddenly got the best of her. Not only did her heart start hammering in her chest, but she also could not stop her brain from thinking how stunning Reggie looked in his suit, standing with the sunshine glinting in his dark brown hair.

She had not noticed the golden shimmers before. It almost seemed like a halo. Now that comparison had her chortling out loud. Reggie was certainly no angel. More like a fallen angel.

So busy had she become with her own thoughts, she failed to notice Reggie had entered the room. When his hip ran into the corner of the table, causing her empty wine goblet to topple and fall to the ground, the breaking of the glass broke through the silence like no other.

"Oh!" Bethany exclaimed, instantly moving forward as if to clean it up herself. Her training at the hotel simply kicked in without conscious thought.

"Don't worry about it," Reggie slurred.

Even as he spoke, the butler moved forward with a couple of pieces of paper. With expert care, he used one piece of paper to transfer the shards onto the other. Without a single word, the mess had been cleared, and they were left alone.

By now, Bethany had come within a couple of feet of Reggie. The smell of alcohol wafted over to her. With a cock of her head and a narrowing of her eyes, she asked, "Are you drunk?"

CHAPTER 7

REGGIE

"Certainly not drunk," Reggie defended himself.

"You can't exactly deny it, Reggie. You reek of a brewery." Looking around for her forgotten purse, she spotted it on the couch. "I think I should go home." Making to move around him, she stopped short as Reggie's hand stopped her.

Reaching out, Reggie could not stop himself. Just the feel of her silky skin under his fingertips caused him to think about more than a simple touch. What would her lips feel like against his? Would she respond to his touch the way he imagined?

"Please stay," Reggie spoke tenderly.

His tone stopped her faster than his touch. Raising her eyes to meet his, she said, "I thought this was supposed to be a business meeting. If I gave you the wrong impression—"

"No," he interrupted her. "You're totally right. I'm sorry if I had to have drinks with a client before meeting with you. It was the only day Andrew was available to meet. I should've stopped after the first beer."

"You're absolutely right about that," Bethany replied, moving closer to Reggie and pulling her arm free.

The warmth of her breath cascaded over his face. He could detect the fruity scent of wine. "It looks like I wasn't the only one imbibing tonight. What did Dillon bring you? I don't recognize it." He enjoyed watching her cheeks flush with her confusion.

"Who's Dillon?"

"The butler." Reggie waved toward where the man had left them.

"Oh. I never did catch his name. Yes, he brought me a glass of Moscato."

"Yes, that's it; now I can place it. Are you ready for dinner? I'm sure Jeff's chomping at the bit to present his culinary masterpiece. You wouldn't want to deny him his delight, would you?"

"Well, when you put it that way." Bethany stepped backward, her calves bumping against the edge of the couch caused her to lose her balance. Before she knew it, she plunked down onto the cushion, her purse instantly catapulting from the cushion and toppling onto the floor.

Reggie watched the scene with amusement. Almost as if in slow motion, the contents of her purse spilled out toward his feet. An inch from his right shoe, a tampon came to rest. Not even attempting to prevent the smile from overtaking his face, he bent forward and picked up the feminine supply, and held it out toward Bethany. Pretending complete ignorance, he said, "I think this is yours."

Bethany's hand snatched the offending article from his fingertips and shoved it unceremoniously into her purse. Without any regard for the other items, she crammed them into her bag and kept her eyes averted from his. "I'm sorry, Reggie. I think I've made a mistake coming here tonight."

"Nonsense. Accidents happen to anyone. Think nothing of it. Leave your stuff here; we can get it later. The dining room is just through here." Reggie reached down and cupped his hand around her elbow, raising her from the couch by sheer force. For such a small woman, she sure could put up a lot of resistance.

"I don't know—"

"Don't make me explain to Jeff how he wasted his effort on tonight's meal," Reggie pleaded, his tone light and pleasant. He enjoyed playing on Bethany's sense of honor.

"Fine." She shoved her purse away from her, heedless of how it landed. "It's not like you don't know everything in there already anyway." Without warning, she strode away from Reggie, leaving him to catch up with her.

"You sure are unpredictable," Reggie muttered.

"What's that?" Turning her head, her eyes narrowed dangerously.

"Nothing. I can't wait to hear what you've come up with for this auction."

"Me?" She stopped short, turning to face him so fast he ran straight into her.

Reggie's entire body collided with hers. Automatically, his hand reached out and grabbed both sides of her waist to prevent her from toppling over. With more force than necessary, he pulled her forward until she once again touched his entire front.

His hands felt like they were on fire. Never before had he wanted to kiss anybody so badly. Looking down at her luscious lips, the tip of his tongue hastily licked his bottom lip as he resisted his initial impulse to drop his head down until his lips met hers. Her next words stopped any amorous thoughts.

"I thought you had the brilliant ideas for tonight's dinner. If you think I'm going to be doing all the work, then you've got another thing coming, mister. Oh, and watch where you're going. I don't appreciate being manhandled."

His hands released her so swiftly; she stumbled away from him. Rather than try to catch her and receive a slap from her, he let her fend for herself. "I didn't mean it as it sounded—I mean—I've got ideas to contribute. We're going to be a team on this. Besides, I think I've got the perfect venue lined up for the event."

"You do?"

The shock on her face was laughable. Reggie could get used to keeping her guessing. Her expressions were just priceless. Rather than answering her, he stepped around her still form to lead the way to the dining room. "Yes. Come. Let's eat and talk about our plans."

He could hear her shoes hitting the tile floor. Unfortunately, the venue was the only good news he had to share; the timing would be a point of contention that he was not anxious to reveal. Maybe they could have another glass of wine and eat before that particular aspect came up. He pointed to a seat for Bethany. "Will this spot do for you?"

"I don't see why not," Bethany replied, stepping forward to move the chair.

Seeing her intention, Reggie beat her to it. He pulled the chair out and waited for her to stand in front of it before he gently pushed it forward until she was comfortably seated.

Feeling pleased with himself, he shrugged out of his jacket while he moved over to the chair at the head of the table. With practiced ease, Dillon stepped forward and took the suit jacket, and left again just as unobtrusively.

"Doesn't that get creepy?" Bethany suddenly asked.

Confused, Reggie asked, "What?"

"Having people jump out of the shadows to be at your beck and call."

"I'd hardly say he was lurking in the shadows. Dillon's been employed here for the last six years. He knows my routine pretty well by now."

"That doesn't answer my question," Bethany muttered, her hands touching the linen napkin and the edges of the silverware as if she were looking for something to do.

"Are you uncomfortable here, Bethany? We could take our meal out to the patio if you'd prefer it."

"No! I mean—I'm sorry. I don't know what's wrong with me." She bit her bottom lip as her cheeks flamed red again. Taking a deep breath, she changed the subject. "So you said you lined up a venue in New York. That's good. So how many months do we have to plan this auction?"

Reggie coughed nervously. This was exactly the question he had been dreading. Just as he opened his mouth to answer, the door to the kitchen swung open, and two wait staff entered the room with steaming plates of food. Almost sighing with relief, Reggie grinned over to Bethany and said, "I think business will have to wait."

Seconds later, a man dressed all in white entered the room. His proud look was clearly evident as he waited for their words of praise at the artistic display of the meal. "You're lucky to have arrived just as they were ready."

"I'll say," Reggie gushed, eager to shift the conversation to something less dangerous. "It appears you've outdone yourself yet again. Thank you, Jeff."

Tipping his head forward, Jeff said, "Let me know if you need anything. The next course will be out shortly." He left the room.

"The next course?" Bethany asked, leaning forward as she whispered her surprise.

"Yes. Jeff never does a simple fare. You're in for at least six courses tonight. I hope you're hungry."

"I'll never be able to eat everything here, let alone another five dishes. Reggie, this is ridiculous."

Chuckling at her, he said, "You don't have to eat everything on your plate. Just sample what looks good, and don't worry about the rest."

"But that's just wasteful."

"If you're worried about starving kids and all that, don't. None of this will go to waste; trust me."

"What do you mean?"

"The dogs usually finish whatever gets left behind. They love Jeff's cooking almost as much as I do."

"Dogs?" Bethany looked around as if expecting the animals to be waiting for scraps under the table.

Another chuckle escaped his lips. "The dogs aren't here. Jeff takes the leftovers to the shelter downtown."

"Oh, that's nice of him." She picked up her fork, ready to get started. Her eyes darted up to Reggie as she added, "And it's nice of you to let him. After all, you pay for all this food."

"Thanks for noticing. If you asked Jeff, I had nothing to do with any of this. That's okay, though. He's the best chef in the nation. Eat up. You'll see what I mean."

Without any further hesitation, Bethany cut into the delicate wedge of salad after dipping the tines of her fork into the small dish of dressing. The subtle flavors from the seasoned dressing were unlike anything she had ever tasted. Her eyes closed in delight.

"It's good, isn't it?" Seeing her nod, he applied himself to his own meal. Just as he had hoped, the conversation about the event's date had been temporarily forgotten. Dinner continued with only small talk between bites of Jeff's masterful food to keep their mouths busy.

Sooner than he would have liked, the last dishes were taken away. Reggie had watched Bethany with renewed appreciation. Unlike the girls he usually entertained, she had eaten almost everything on every plate. Even though she was as thin as the models who regularly starved themselves, Bethany somehow found somewhere to put all the food.

As she sat back, her hands resting across her stomach, she moaned, "I don't think I'll need to eat for a week. It was all so wonderful; I couldn't stop myself. Be sure to pass along my compliments to Jeff. He truly is a master of seasoning."

"Thank you, ma'am." Jeff had managed to appear without either of them noticing.

After her initial start of surprise, Bethany turned to smile warmly at the chef. "I meant every word. I don't think I've ever tasted any food that was so good. Although, I feel bad for eating everything. Now the dogs won't have as much to eat."

Reggie reached out and patted her arm. Her care for the dogs was touching. "Don't worry; I'll make an extra donation to make up for it."

"You'd do that?"

"Certainly. I don't want you to curb your appetite because of a misplaced belief that you're keeping it from someone or something else. What good is all my money if I can't contribute to the charities which matter?"

"I never thought about it like that. Thank you, Reggie." She picked up her third glass of wine, her head already swimming, but she needed to cover her confusion. "You're really nothing like I thought you were," she admitted before tipping the glass up to her lips.

Not sure what to make of her admission, he sat back and contemplated her. Could it be that she felt the same for him as he felt for her? "Would you care to elaborate on that?" Reggie leaned forward, eager to get to the bottom of this. Having her be slightly tipsy might be his only opportunity to get a straight answer out of her.

"Not really." She set her glass down, her gaze leveling with his. "So, tell me about this venue."

"I was hoping to avoid this for a while longer."

"Avoid what? I thought you were excited about the place you found. Don't tell me it's outside of New York City. You know it'll be less profitable if people have to get transportation that far."

"No. It's not that. The location couldn't be better."

"Then what's the problem?"

"The only time it was available was in twenty-eight days." Reggie's admission came at the exact wrong time. Bethany had just taken another sip of her wine. Within seconds, his shirt was spattered with the sweet liquid as Bethany sputtered and tried to compose herself again.

"Are you kidding?" She rose from the table; her eyes hardened in anger as she leaned her fists against the wooden surface.

CHAPTER 8

BETHANY

"We'll just have to reschedule it," Bethany declared, her mind reeling with plans. Nobody could possibly expect her to plan a profitable charity auction in less than a month. It just was not possible. Nor was it practical. She knew it was a mistake letting Reggie have any part of this project. Men just did not understand the importance of the details.

"That's not happening. I'm telling you, this is the perfect venue. Unless you want to wait until winter, then we'll just have to buckle down and make it work."

"I don't think you appreciate the work which still needs to be done. I mean—everything still needs to be handled. We've gotten exactly nothing done to this point. We don't even have a guest list, for pity's sake."

Pushing away from the table, she needed to get some distance from Reggie before she did more than just spit wine on him. She paced the side of the dining room with angry steps. If she had not chosen flats, she would have thrown off the heels so she could stomp her feet on the ground to help vent her frustration.

The nerve of the man. How could he put her in such an awful position? This was her first task with the charity group, and he was already setting her up for failure. She knew there was a reason she hated Reggie all of these years.

Just as the thought came to her, she rounded onto Reggie. "You did this on purpose, didn't you? Here you show up at my hotel begging me to have dinner with you. Then you show up late and drunk to boot. I should've known you're still up to your old tricks. And I fell for it again!"

Having said her piece, she turned and stomped out of the room. If only she had her own car! Another mistake on her part. Never again would she be at Reggie's complete mercy. She had really done it to herself this time. Never again!

By the time she made it back to her purse, she had already planned to just walk out the front door and call a driver as soon as she got off the property. No way was she going to stick around to be ridiculed further. Her feet pounded the floor, muffled slightly by the plush Persian rug in the formal sitting room.

Reaching down, she grabbed up her purse. Several items flew from the side, yet she no longer cared about what they were or where they ended up. Reggie could keep whatever it was as a souvenir for all she cared.

Tucking the purse up under her arm, she turned only to be stopped short by Reggie's body. His arms were crossed high up on his chest as he held his ground. "Are you through having your little tantrum?"

"Get out of my way, you brute. I'm going home. It was a mistake coming here. I should never have trusted you to be anything but a loser."

"Hardly becoming, Bethany. If you'd let me explain, we could clear all of this up before you say anything more that you don't mean."

Tipping her chin until she could glare up at him, she said, "Oh, trust me; I meant every word I said. Now move!"

"What're you going to do? Walk home?"

"Cute. Since you're not gentlemanly enough to have your driver take me home, I'll call myself a car. But I won't be sitting here in your home while I wait." Bethany attempted to step around Reggie only to be stopped by his arm flinging out in front of her.

She hastily stepped back as if his arm would burn her skin if she came into contact with it. "Don't make this any uglier, Reggie. If you don't let me leave this house, then I'll scream until the staff comes running."

"Don't tempt me, Bethany. You're not going anywhere until you hear me out."

Feeling the last of her patience drain away, she inhaled deeply, ready to let the most piercing scream escape. In her mind, it would rival the best horror films in its volume. Just as the first of her breath left her mouth, she felt herself suddenly being flung.

In an instant, Reggie had managed to flip her around until her back rested against his chest with his arm pinning her tightly to him while his other hand clamped down over her mouth. Struggling to free herself, she had no idea how this had gone so terribly wrong, yet she could not seem to make any headway toward escaping his crushing grasp.

Leaning his mouth until it almost touched her ear, Reggie spoke calmly. "Stop fighting me, Bethany. I don't want to hurt you. I'm going to hire as many people as we need to make sure this event is a huge success. You won't have to lift a finger if you don't want to, but I'll be sure to give you more than half of the credit.

"Are you listening to me, Bethany? I'm not scheming, and I'm not trying to hurt you. Stop wiggling! You're only hurting yourself."

Reggie's words finally sank in, and all of the fight left her in an instant. Her sudden change almost caused Reggie to drop her. She should have tried this tactic first. Her self-defense coach would have been so disappointed at her initial reaction.

"Are you going to calm down?" Reggie asked evenly.

Bethany nodded.

"I'm going to remove my hand from your mouth. Do you promise not to scream?"

Another nod made Reggie finally release her mouth, but he still held her tightly to his body. Only then did her mind register how close they were to one another. Heat flushed through her body. More flustered than she cared to admit, she simply said, "Let me go, Reggie."

Faster than she would have cared to admit, Reggie complied with her wishes. She stepped away from him, missing the feel of his body instantly. Inhaling to get her bearings, she could smell his musky scent all around her, further confusing her brain.

How had this happened? Wasn't she furious with him? How had he managed to diffuse her anger and make her feel like she wanted to kiss him so easily? It must have been the wine. She could have sworn he had said he wanted to help her succeed with this project.

"I've got to go home."

"Bethany, don't."

His simple statement forced her to look up into his eyes. Could there be something brewing between them other than her anger? She no longer trusted her instincts where he was concerned. Too many emotions had passed through her in the last several minutes. She needed some space to clear her mind.

"I need to get some air." Glancing for an escape route, she felt trapped and ready to run.

"Fine, let's take a walk through the grounds. I can tell you what I had in mind for staffing the auction."

"Fine," she repeated back to him, feeling foolish for her earlier display.

Reggie reached out toward her but paused as she flinched away from him. Shifting his hand, he pointed to the doors on the other end of the room. "We can go out through there."

Bethany's mind did not hesitate with his choice of escape. She turned and charged through the room, not waiting to see if Reggie followed her. Flinging the door open, she inhaled the fresh air to clear Reggie's sexy smell from her mind. How could he have such an effect on her? How could her body betray her by wanting *him*?

"Tell me your great plans then," she curtly spoke, hating her own tone but unable to take it back. Up ahead, she could see several pathways through the garden. Her feet moved of their own accord.

Reggie remained silent for a few seconds. Bethany wondered if she had managed to catch him in another lie. Maybe he did not have a plan at all.

"I told Shannon today that I'd be taking the next few weeks off so I could devote all my time to this project. If you don't believe me, go ahead and call her right now." Reggie raised his eyebrows in challenge.

Bethany's eyes narrowed suspiciously, yet she kept herself from taking up his dare. She was not going to give him the satisfaction. When she got home, she would call Shannon and see if their stories matched.

"Let's just say that I believe you. Who's going to take care of your business? I thought you had an important project brewing right now."

"I do. I'm going to have Adam take the lead on it. He's been chomping at the bit for an opportunity like this, so I'm going to let him give it a go."

"Just like that, huh? A deal to double the size of your company, and you're going to hand over the reins to someone else. I think that's careless, don't you?"

"I'm telling you that this project is more important than anything to me right now. What'll it take for me to convince you?"

"Fine." Bethany crossed her arms over her chest as if to defend herself against his truth. "What's this great plan of yours?"

"As I said before, while you were fighting me like a wild banshee, I'm going to hire the best event planners, and we're going to let them do their thing. You and I can free up our time to go over the guest lists and gather the auction items. I've already got some pretty decent leads on some cool things to feature."

"Really? Do share."

"Nope. Not until you apologize."

Bethany pursed her lips and shook her head. Almost without thought, her arms crossed over her middle as if she were protecting herself from another onslaught. "I'm not ready to apologize, not after you manhandled me as you did."

"I'm sorry, Bethany. Truly, I am. I couldn't have you screaming and scaring my staff. What else was I supposed to do?"

Feeling foolish about taking her stance against him, she turned away, her eyes not even seeing the beautiful scenery around them. Conflicting emotions warred within her as she tried to reconcile her anger at him for grabbing her and wishing he would do it again.

What was wrong with her? Had Pete really messed her up emotionally for life? Would she ever feel normal being alone with another man? She honestly hoped so, if only so she could begin to have peace and tranquility again.

Breathing in deeply, she turned to apologize, only to discover herself quite alone. Where had Reggie gone? How had she been so engrossed in her own thoughts that she had not even heard him leaving?

Continuing to turn, she spotted a movement off to her right. Deciding to investigate, she started moving forward. "Reggie?" she called out, hoping he would reappear up ahead.

Silence greeted her. Then she started to listen more intently. The stillness here was nothing like out at her place. She could hear the leaves rustling in the trees overhead. The titters of birds sounded off in the distance as well as the splashing of water, probably from the fountain out front.

Bethany felt herself relax even though she wondered why Reggie would have left her. Of course, he had every right to leave after the treatment she had given him. She could hardly blame him for wanting to be away from her. Heck, she often felt the same way about herself these days.

She continued to walk up the pathway, not really knowing if she was heading in the right direction. It did not really matter, she enjoyed the solace, yet she wanted to apologize to Reggie. It seemed she kept making a fool of herself lately, and she did not like the way it changed who she ultimately was to those around her.

With this shocking thought still fresh in her mind, she hardly even registered the sight in front of her. Rounding a bend in the path, her eyes traveled up to a fenced-in enclosure. Just inside the fine wire, she spotted several spotted hens pecking happily at the ground.

With a squeal of delight, she rushed forward and kneeled at the edge of the enclosure. Never would she have suspected Reggie of wanting to own chickens. Maybe they were for his staff; it just did not ring true for Reggie to want to own them himself. He seemed far too carefree.

Just as she had convinced herself that the staff owned them, Reggie came around the back corner of the fancy chicken coop. In his hands, he held a beautiful Banty hen. The hen rested easily and comfortably in his arms while his hand stroked her head gently.

"Are these birds yours?" she blurted without thinking. Even the tone of her voice came out sharper than she intended. Luckily, he seemed too preoccupied with the hen to notice.

"Yes. This one is named Fluffy."

"Seriously? I have a rooster named Fluffy."

"You own chickens? How strange. Why would you name a rooster Fluffy?"

"Well, when I named him, I thought he was a hen. I didn't have the heart to rename him when he turned out to be a boy. Besides, it seemed kind of funny, so I left it. Pete—" Flustered that she would even bring up his name in Reggie's presence caused her to turn away and chastise herself.

"What about Pete? You know you can talk about him with me. I read the article in the paper. I'm sorry things didn't work out for the two of you."

"That's an understatement. Thank you for understanding about him."

"I don't really."

"You don't what?" Only half of Bethany's mind was on their conversation, the other half being preoccupied with the revelation of the chickens in Reggie's immaculate yard.

"I don't understand why you and Pete broke up. I mean, did you get cold feet?"

Scoffing out loud despite herself, she kneeled again to put her finger inside the coop as several chickens came to investigate whether or not she had any food to offer. "I found out Pete slept with my Maid of Honor the night before our wedding. If I hadn't accidentally overheard her conversation, I would have walked up the aisle and married the cheating bastard. He didn't have the courage to fess up, and he would have let me marry him even knowing what he did."

Wondering at Reggie's silence, she chanced a glance up at him. He had turned, leaving her with only a view of his profile. His hand no longer stroked the chicken but remained poised just over her head as his fingers clenched into a fist. She saw a tightening of the muscles around his mouth and asked, "What're you thinking?"

"That I'd like to put my fist through Pete's perfect teeth."

"You'd have to get in line. If he dared to show up again, my dad would beat you to it. Of course, Dad didn't know about the issue when I called off the wedding. I only told him a few days ago. Pete had already moved out of our house. I can only assume he moved in with his new girlfriend."

"You can't be serious."

"No. But I don't care at this point. Pete's out of my life." Deciding to change to a safer topic, she added, "I'd like to apologize for the way I acted earlier. I was childish and rude. I said things out of anger, which should never have been spoken. Will you forgive me?"

"Already done. I shouldn't have ever grabbed you as I did. It probably scared you." His hand opened and resumed petting Fluffy. "Do you want to hold her?" he asked, holding out the clucking hen toward her.

"I'd love to," she answered, swiftly standing beside him and holding out her hands. Maybe Reggie wasn't the villain she had made him out to be. After all, how bad could he be if he had a hen named Fluffy?

CHAPTER 9

REGGIE

His thoughts of revenge against Pete were interrupted when Bethany's voice sounded. So caught up in his own mind, he entirely missed what she had said. "What was that?"

"I asked you why you had chickens." Her upturned face seemed relaxed and peaceful as she stroked Fluffy's soft feathers.

"It's silly, really. We should head back to the house. Since you pointed out, we've only got a few short weeks to get this auction together." Reggie held out his hands for Fluffy to be returned to him.

She turned her body, preventing him from accessing the bird. "Nope, not until you give me a real reason why you'd want chickens. It's not like owning a dog. You've got to have a story behind it."

"What if I do? Maybe I'm not ready to talk about it with you." Reggie's clipped words escaped before he could filter their content. As soon as he spoke them, he wished he could take them back. Bethany's expression turned sad, and she hastily turned to face him, holding out Fluffy without another comment.

"I'm sorry if I overstepped," she whispered.

As soon as Reggie took the bird, she turned and walked away. "I'll meet you back at the house," she called over her shoulder, her hurried steps swiftly taking her away from him.

Wishing he could just run after her, he realized the moments apart might allow him to decide what he wanted to share with her. Did he really want to tell her the truth? Would she laugh at him if he did? Was it worth the risk?

Maybe. Reggie brought Fluffy up so he could rub his cheek against her silky feathers. The smoothness always seemed to calm him when he was particularly confused or upset. Right now, he felt both emotions, but confusion seemed to be warring for top billing.

How could Bethany have infiltrated his life so completely that he would consider sharing his darkest secrets with her? Only the day before, his life had been so simple. Lonely, to be sure, but simple nonetheless.

Within minutes, Reggie had returned Fluffy to the coop and returned to the house. As soon as he entered the formal sitting room, he noticed Bethany had taken her purse and disappeared. He sprinted forward, hoping she had not had a chance to get too far before he could have an opportunity to explain himself.

Just as he entered the foyer, he happened to see the door latch just finish turning. She had tried to be stealthily quiet, but he had seen it. Charging forward, he grabbed the handle and twisted it, pulling the door open with enough force for it to hit the wall behind it and spring back to hit him in the heels.

Heedless of the sharp pain, he stepped outside again. Bethany had moved over to the fountain, her cell phone up against her ear. Reggie panicked, thinking she was planning on leaving so soon. "Bethany!" he called out, louder than was necessary but wanting to stop her from completing her call.

Seeing her jump in fright, Reggie wished he could start this whole evening over. It seemed as if everything which could go wrong was happening. Could he fix this before she decided he was no different than he had been throughout school? More than ever, he wanted to prove her wrong.

Even as the thought came to his mind, he wondered at this new turn of events. What could happen between the two of them? Did he want something to spark with her?

Yes! His mind called out decisively, surprising himself at the force of it.

Bethany turned, the phone falling away from her ear. "I was just calling a car. It seems as though we're getting off on the wrong foot here, and I thought it might be best to call it an evening."

"I wish you wouldn't," Reggie spoke softly, his long strides bringing him to a stop directly in front of her. "I'd like to tell you about the chickens."

"No, Reggie. You don't have to share that with me just because I threw a tantrum. It wouldn't be right."

"Did you finish calling for a car?"

"No."

"Good! Come with me," Reggie said, his eagerness at her answer causing him to forget how jumpy she could get. As soon as his hand took her arm, he felt her tense up. As if he had been shocked, his fingers dropped from her skin, and he stepped back. "I'm sorry, Beth. I keep forgetting to go slowly with you."

Her eyes narrowed as she looked up at him. "What does that mean exactly? I'm not a wilting flower that needs to be coddled."

"It's just—I don't know what I'm trying to say. Nothing I do seems right around you, but I'd like to try to change that." He stepped back to give her more space as he sucked in a hasty breath. "Would you be so kind as to accompany me back to the house? We've got a party to plan."

"A party? This, coming from the ultimate party boy." Bethany raised one eyebrow. "Fine. I'll come back, but I shouldn't stay too much longer."

"Do you have plans for later tonight?" Reggie turned and started walking back toward the house. His attempt at light conversation still sounded stilted to his own ears.

"Maybe."

"Let me guess. You have a date with your chickens?"

Bethany burst out laughing.

Caught off guard at the beautiful sound, he frowned and looked over at her.

"Busted!"

Reggie's chuckling joined in with hers. At least they were getting along now. That was a step in the right direction. Now, if only he could prevent himself from putting his foot in his mouth for the rest of the evening. Only then might they actually start getting somewhere in repairing their long-dead friendship.

BETHANY

Thinking back on their conversation, Bethany realized Reggie had called her by her old nickname. For some reason, that term of endearment caused her to soften even more to him than she normally would have. Maybe he felt something more about her than she had realized.

He certainly had a soft side she would not have expected. Hopefully, he would share the story of his chickens before the night was over. If not, she would not push him.

They returned to the house, but instead of going to the formal sitting room, Reggie led the way down the long hallway to a room at the back of the house. This space had darker walls and large, comfortable chairs. "Is this a home theater?" she asked, her eyes taking in the enormous empty wall and the projector hanging from the ceiling.

"Yes. It's a guilty pleasure of mine. I like sitting in here. It calms my mind." Reggie walked to the back row of plush chairs and sat down on the edge of it.

The look he gave her warmed her heart. She could easily see him as a ten-year-old again. Taking the chair next to him, her hand rested on the silky-soft leather. He certainly liked the finer things in life. This was nothing like the beat-up La-Z-Boy chair she had in her living room.

Not that she would dare to compare her life with his. While he had been brought up to expect everything to be the best of the best, her parents had taught her to be frugal. Every cent they earned had gone back into making improvements in the family's hotel business. Not that she minded, she knew it was her legacy.

"What're you thinking?" Reggie asked softly, his voice not carrying far in the well-insulated room.

"That you and I were brought up quite differently from one another."

"How so?"

Bethany raised her eyebrows as she gestured to the entire room and house in general. "All this."

"What about it?"

"That's just it; you don't see how grand all of this is. I'm sure my quaint little house would seem like a run-down shack to you."

"I don't care about all of this."

Bethany rolled her eyes.

"Okay, I enjoy my things, but it isn't everything. I only bought this house because I knew my parents expected it of me. If I had my choice, I would've picked a cabin beside the lake, so I could drink my coffee while watching the birds dive into the water."

"Really? You'd give all of this up?"

"In a heartbeat. They're just things. I want something real."

"Like what? I mean, besides the cabin. What else do you want?"

"A relationship. A real relationship."

"You have girls over here all the time."

"That's not the same, and you know it. I know they're only here for the money. If I were dirt poor, they wouldn't give me a second glance."

Glancing from the corner of her eyes, Bethany wondered why he had become morose so swiftly. With as handsome as he was, he certainly sold himself short. If it had not been for his family's money, he could have made a career as a model or even an actor. Of that, she was certain. Wanting to know more about what he was thinking, she asked, "What makes you say that?"

"I did a little experiment one summer while I was in college. I packed a backpack and went hiking in Europe. I didn't tell anyone who I was, and if anyone asked, I told them I was an unemployed college dropout. Nobody gave me the time of day, let alone a lift, when I really needed one. It gave me quite an eye-opening experience."

"So you're saying money makes all the difference?"

"No, I'm saying money makes life easier, but it doesn't bring happiness in the way you'd expect."

"I see." Bethany picked at a thread sticking out of a hole in her jeans.

"Do you?"

"I think so." She sat back in the plush chair, her expression growing introspective as she tried to imagine why he would feel so lonely. Suddenly a thought struck her. "Why the cabin?"

Caught off guard, he did not answer right away. "What?"

"You had a pretty clear picture of the cabin you would rather live in. Is it a real place?" Her eyes searched his for the hidden meaning.

Reggie jumped up from his chair, pacing away from her with sharp steps.

She must have struck a sensitive subject. Rather than excuse herself, she waited in silence. If they were going to work together, she needed to get to know him better. This might be the perfect opportunity to find out.

"Yes. It was a real place. But it's gone now. A flood washed it away."

"Oh, that's terrible. Was it someplace you used to visit?"

"Yes. I don't really want to talk about this right now." Turning back to face her, his eyes squinting as it appeared he tried to keep them from tearing up. In an instant, he returned to his seat and said, "I'd like to tell you about the auction items I've lined up already."

Reeling from his sudden shift in both mood and conversation, she let the matter go for the moment. "Sure. It'll give me an idea of the direction we need to go for procuring more items."

"The first is a weekend away in a luxury treehouse."

"Okay, that's strange. Isn't that an oxymoron? I mean, how can a treehouse also be luxurious?"

"Oh, it's absolutely amazing. My friend, Markson, has funded a whole neighborhood of treehouses up in the Catskills. He assured me that the experience would be one-of-a-kind. I trust his opinion implicitly."

"Alrighty then. What else do you have?"

"A rare car."

"How rare?"

"Only two in existence."

"Someone is donating that for the charity? Who?"

"An anonymous donor. I promised to keep it a secret."

"Even from me?"

"Yep. That was the deal. Nobody could know."

"Well, the buyer will know. The owner's name would be on the title."

"Nope. It was bought through a private LLC."

"Hmm. Quite mysterious. Great job on that score, though. Although, I wish I could thank him myself for his generosity."

"I'll be sure to pass it along."

"So, I'm right about it being a man?" She cocked her head playfully.

"I never said I agreed with you, only that I'd pass the compliment along."

"Hmm. That's true."

"Don't try to get it out of me. Not even a tickle war would get me to spill the beans."

"Oh really? Are you sure about that?" Bethany pushed her clawed fingers toward him menacingly, devilishly smiling as she did so.

"Hey!" Reggie jumped up again. This time laughter bubbled from his lips as he kept himself out of her reach.

Bethany much preferred this side of him than any other she had seen so far. Maybe there was more to him than she realized. She just might give him a chance to be her friend after all. It was the least she could do given the circumstances in which they had found themselves.

Chapter 10

Bethany

The phone ringing inside the house caused Bethany to break into a run. Only having heard it by chance while out feeding the chickens, she hoped it would be Reggie. Even as the thought struck her mind, it almost caused her to trip over the top step of the porch. Since when did she run to the phone to talk to a boy? Not since she was a teenager.

Fearing whoever was calling would give up before she reached the receiver, she flung herself inside the house and made a mad leap for the phone resting on the kitchen counter. More than a little breathless, she hastily punched the button to pick up the call and brought it up to her ear.

"Hello?" she managed to gasp out.

"Bethany?" Shannon asked. "Are you okay?"

"Yes. I just ran to get the phone."

"It sounds like you were expecting someone else. Dare I venture to guess you were hoping it was Reggie?" she teased.

"You can't be serious!" she denied instantly, yet her sense of humor caught up to her, and she chuckled. "Maybe a little," she admitted sheepishly. "Hey! What're you doing calling me? Aren't you at work?"

"Look at the clock, silly. It's noon. I get to take lunches, you know."

Doing just that, Bethany looked over at the microwave and saw it was exactly noon. "Anxious much?"

"Are you kidding? With the mood Reggie's been in this morning, I've been dying to find out what happened at his house last night!"

"That bad, huh?"

"What? No way. He's had a permanent smile on his face, and he's been whistling in his office. Do you know how many times I've heard him whistle?"

"I give up. How many?"

"Never!"

Biting her bottom lip, Bethany rushed to sit down in the chair at the kitchen table. "I thought maybe I messed things up really bad. Tell me everything!"

"You can't be serious. I'm not saying anything until you tell me every little detail about your evening. Were the flowers nice?"

Chuckling, Bethany said, "I should've known those were your idea. What else did you plan?"

"Nothing."

"Right!"

"I swear. In fact, even the flowers weren't my idea. Reggie just had me place the order. Now, I've only got thirty minutes, so you better start talking, missy!"

As if the floodgates opened, the words gushed out of Bethany's mouth. Once again, she felt like a schoolgirl who was having her first crush. The feelings she had grew more intense as she told her best friend about everything.

When the story came to a close, Shannon asked, "He really grabbed you like that?"

"Yes! It made me so mad!" The intense feeling seemed to reignite inside of her as she thought about it again.

"Are you sure it was just anger? You can't tell me you didn't like it a little bit. I mean, come on! Reggie's a complete hottie. Certainly, you didn't miss that."

"I'm not a complete moron. Of course, I noticed. But—."

"But what?" Shannon pressed.

Bethany could imagine Shannon sitting with the phone pressed tightly to her ear as she waited for her final admission.

"But I can't be with Reggie. I mean—all those years of torture."

"Was it really that bad? How much worse was what Pete did to you?"

"True. I guess it's just turned into a habit not to like him. He's actually a pretty decent guy when he's just himself." She sighed, wondering if she should ask Shannon the question which had been troubling her the most.

"Okay, spill it."

Caught off guard, Bethany asked, "Spill what?"

"Whatever you've got rolling around in that brain of yours."

"Fine. Has Reggie ever mentioned anything about a cabin to you before?"

"Hmm. I don't think so," Shannon replied right away before growing silent. The sound of her breath through the phone grew louder as she walked back to the office. "Wait, I think he did say something once. I think he said he used to visit his grandparents at their cabin when he was really little. I might be wrong, but I think that's what I recall."

"Hmm. That sounds about right. Do you know if his grandparents live around here?"

"Not a clue. Reggie doesn't really talk about his family much. I don't think they're very close."

"Really? I mean, he's running the family business. I would've thought they'd be pretty tight."

"Nope. His dad's on the board of directors, but he doesn't even stop in to talk with Reggie when the meetings adjourn. It's kinda weird, don't you think?"

"Maybe." Bethany's mind raced through the little details Reggie had let drop the night before. She wanted to ask more questions, but it sounded like Shannon's lunch was almost over. "Are you heading back into the office?"

"Yes. I'm just waiting for the elevator right now. Why?"

"Do you want to get dinner or something?"

"Are you asking me out?"

"Yeah, that's my thing now. Didn't you know?"

Shannon chuckled at her strange sense of humor. "Sure. I'm free tonight. Besides, I'm not done grilling you about last night."

"Ugh."

"Hey, this girl can only live vicariously through your exciting life."

"Yeah, that's my life summed up perfectly! See you tonight at five. I'll pick you up."

"Sounds good. Bye."

No sooner had she hung up the phone than she jumped up from the chair and left the kitchen. Rushing into the living room, she seated herself on the couch and pulled her laptop open. She had a few hours to do some extensive research on Reggie's family. There was a story hidden there, and if he would not tell her, then she would find out on her own.

REGGIE

Every time he thought about the evening before, he could not help but smile. More than once, he caught himself whistling some cheery nonsensical tune. Rather than shut it off immediately, he let the tune play itself out before reapplying himself to the tasks set before him for the day.

Unfortunately, his concentration kept warping back to how he felt about Bethany rather than on work. It really was a good thing Adam was going to be taking over this project right now. If it were left up to him in this state of mind, he would blow the deal for sure.

What was it about Bethany that captured him so completely? Was it because Pete cheated on her? Or was it something more than that? Certainly, he hated to see women treated poorly, but he thought there was more to it than that.

Thinking back to the feel of her in his arms as she struggled to get away caused him to start whistling another jaunty tune. Her strength had surprised him. It was almost as if she had some training in self-defense. For some reason, that idea pleased him even more. He hated wilting flowers. He much preferred her self-sufficiency.

Thinking even more about the things he liked about her, he realized he wanted to see her again. As soon as possible. Could he find an excuse to see her? Maybe he could take dinner to her house, and they could talk about the auction while they ate. After all, it had worked last night.

Liking this idea more and more, he tapped his fingers on the edge of his keyboard. Putting action to his thoughts, he typed out a query for nearby restaurants which could deliver to his office. Within a few minutes, he settled on an Italian restaurant.

Before he could talk himself out of it, he ordered enough food to feed a small army. Since he really did not know what she preferred, he basically ordered one of everything on the menu. When he paid the seven hundred dollar bill, he began to wonder how he was going to get all the food over to her house.

Only then did he realize he did not know her home address. Suddenly nervous, he launched himself up from his chair with enough force to throw the wheeled chair back against the wall behind him. Crossing his office, he threw open his door and looked out at Shannon's empty desk.

Where could she have gone? How come she was gone? Looking down at his watch, he realized it was 12:29 pm. Growling in frustration, he hoped she would be back shortly. Rather than wait for her return, he strode over to her desk and began sifting through the Rolodex on her table. He had reached the H section when a voice froze him in his tracks.

"Can I help you find something?" Shannon asked, leaning her hip against the edge of the desk right in front of him.

"Yes. I need Bethany's address."

"Really? Why?"

"We're working on the auction together. Why wouldn't I need her address?" Feeling both foolish and defensive, he failed to notice the smile growing on Shannon's face.

"Are you sending documents to her?"

"No, I thought I'd surprise her with dinner at her house. That way, we could go over our plans without any interruptions." Reggie snapped his mouth shut, wondering why he felt the need to explain himself to his secretary. He tapped his fingers on the desk impatiently, his eyes finally coming to rest on Shannon's.

Only then did he see her humored look. Feeling even more foolish, he hastily turned and headed back to his office, slamming the door behind him as he went. He could have sworn he heard Shannon chuckling behind him, but he could not be certain.

He paced his office for a few minutes before he opted to return to his desk. Just as he seated himself, his hands poised over his keyboard, a knock sounded on his door. "Come in!" He did not look up as he opened another search window on his computer. If he could not get the address from Shannon, then he'd hire a detective to get it for him.

A hand slapping down on his desk caught him by surprise. "Here's her address. You better not hurt her." Shannon's voice was colder than he had ever heard before. Watching her march angrily out of his office, he wondered if he owed her an apology. He knew the two women were friends, but to hear his secretary be so protective of her caught him off guard.

"Noted!" he called after her, just as the door to his office clicked shut. He picked up the note and typed the address directly into his phone.

The afternoon dragged by abominably slowly, especially as he glanced at the clock on his computer every few minutes. By the time it clicked over to 4:20 pm, he had had enough. His productivity was already in the toilet, so he powered down his computer and grabbed his jacket from the peg on the wall.

He left his office, drawing the door closed behind him. "I'm heading out for the day," he announced to Shannon. "If any emergencies come up, forward them to Adam."

"Are you going to Bethany's house?"

"Yes, after I pick up some food."

"Did you call her first? She might already have plans for the night, you know." Shannon leaned back in her chair, a small smile playing at the corners of her mouth.

"Well, no. Um, I don't actually have her phone number. I forgot to get it from her last night."

"I see. Well, good luck then."

Feeling even more uncertain about his plan, he nodded curtly before turning to go to the elevator. He hoped Shannon would have offered Bethany's phone number with his not-so-subtle hint. It appeared Shannon was going to make him work for everything where Bethany was concerned.

He was up for the challenge.

Not twenty minutes later, Reggie had the massive food order loaded into his car. Normally not one to have food in his car, he started to feel more foolish than ever to have bought so much. Shannon's comments also began to work into the worry his brain decided to manufacture. What if Bethany told him to leave?

By the time he pulled up in front of her house, he almost convinced himself to drive away and forget the whole plan. He could always donate the food to a local homeless shelter.

When he glanced over toward the house and saw the white picket fence, his resolve to see this mission through returned. The quaint house reminded him of his grandparents. Surely, that was a sign that he was doing the right thing. Right?

Not wanting to give himself more time to reconsider, he pushed open the driver's door and stepped out of the vehicle. He gathered several bags into both hands and shut the door with his hip. The feeling of coming home persisted as he passed through the narrow gate and stepped onto the flagstone path.

Using his elbow, he touched the doorbell and stepped back to wait for Bethany to answer. He did not have long to wait. The door opened, revealing Bethany wearing a bathrobe and a towel wrapped over her wet hair.

"What're you doing here?" she demanded, her tone more surprised than angry.

Holding up the bags unnecessarily, he said, "I thought we could have another working dinner." A goofy smile lifted the corners of his mouth as his eyes devoured her radiant, natural beauty.

"Oh no," Bethany sighed. She held open the screen door and said, "You might as well come inside."

Not quite the response he hoped for, he entered the house. His eyes roamed as he took in the homey decorations. This was exactly what he loved. A real home.

CHAPTER 11

BETHANY

Not one to worry overmuch about her physical appearance, Bethany patted the towel on her head self-consciously. She stepped back into her house, wondering what she was going to do about her date with Shannon. Hopefully, she'd be understanding about the last-minute cancelation.

"I hope I'm not interrupting anything," Reggie called out over his shoulder. He had headed into the kitchen to set the bags down on the small table off to the side.

"Well, as a matter of fact, I did have plans. Give me a few minutes, and I'll clear my schedule. You really should've called."

"It would've been easier had you given me your phone number," he retorted.

"I guess that would've helped." She laughed as she shook her head. Turning, she left Reggie alone so she could rush back to her room and call Shannon. As soon as she shut the door to her bedroom, she lunged for the phone and hastily dialed. As soon as Shannon picked up, she said, "You're never going to guess who showed up at my doorstep."

"I know. I gave him your address."

"Sorry to cancel on you."

"I'm not. You're going to have so much more to talk about the next time we catch up. Besides, you would have fretted over it all afternoon. Now, get off the phone with me and go talk with him."

"I wish you would've warned me. I opened the door in nothing but a robe and towel."

"Sounds a bit forward, even for you!"

"Ha, ha. Very funny. Talk to you later." Bethany dropped the phone on the charger and raced to her closet. The robe dropped to the floor as she found an appropriate outfit to wear.

She felt so ill-equipped to have male visitors. All of her clothes were either too dressy or entirely too casual. Deciding she had no other choice, she pulled on a pair of sweatpants and her favorite t-shirt, although she did opt for her frilly underclothes, not that he would have an opportunity to see them.

Feeling more nervous than she should in her own house, she dallied in front of the mirror longer than was actually necessary. Not bothering to dry her hair, she simply pulled a brush through her long, straight locks until they were smooth down her back. If he wanted her to be fancier, he should have made better arrangements.

Being snarky was not a good fit for her. She chided herself for even thinking such thoughts. Realizing she was only stalling now, she decided it was time to leave the sanctuary of her room and face whatever Reggie had in mind for her this evening.

When she came to her living room, she spotted Reggie sitting on her couch staring at her open computer. Instantly, her cheeks flushed a deep red as she realized what he must be reading on the screen. While she had not found much on Reggie's family history, the last thing she had found was still displayed. Clearing her throat, she made her presence known.

"Dinner smells wonderful," she spoke casually, hoping to draw his attention away from the computer.

"Were you reading about my family?" he asked, not turning away from the screen.

Groaning inwardly, she stepped over to the edge of the couch. Deciding immediately to come clean, she admitted,

"Yes. I knew you didn't want to talk about your past, and I didn't want to make you uncomfortable. I decided to see what I could find on my own. I'm sorry if I was invading your privacy."

"I can hardly blame you. After all, anything on the internet is a public record. I could hardly stop you." Turning, he stood up as he took in her changed appearance. Yet another side of her came out with her casual clothing and wet hair. "Come on. I hope you're hungry."

Bethany followed him into the kitchen, where she could only stare at boxes and boxes of food set on every available surface. "What is all this? There's enough here to feed an army. Are you expecting a crew of people to be joining us?" Instantly, she felt disappointed at the idea of sharing his time with other people.

"No. I just didn't know what you'd like, so I ordered one of everything on the menu."

"You're not serious!" she exclaimed, finally taking her eyes away from the food to glance over at his face. Seeing the answer clearly written in his expression, she amended, "Of course you are. Okay, I can see we need to set some ground rules for future dinners."

"I like the sound of that," Reggie said, picking up a plate he had found in the cupboard and handing it to Bethany.

Rolling her eyes, Bethany took the plate and began peeking into the boxes until she found the selections she preferred. As she dished it up, she said, "If you're ever uncertain, just order a hamburger and pineapple pizza for me. If you don't like pizza—"

"I do. That sounds amazing. What else?" Reggie interrupted. His fingers grazed against hers as he grabbed the serving spoon in the risotto as she let go of it.

Feeling flustered at the contact, she shook her head and dismissed any other food ideas instantly. "I'm giving you my phone number so we can coordinate our plans easier." Gesturing at the vast quantities of food, she added, "I can't have you doing this craziness every night."

"I like doing crazy. It's kind of a specialty of mine," he murmured over her shoulder, his breath tickling the edge of her ear.

His proximity sent shivers of excitement all through her. Biting her lip to keep from sighing, she moved sideways to get out of his way. How could he have changed so completely in only forty-eight hours? Her body certainly had its own ideas about being around him.

"What would you like to know?"

His soft voice broke into her internal dialogue. "I'm sorry. What?"

"Your research about me. What would you like to know?" He repeated.

Feeling like a child being called out by a teacher for passing notes, she shrugged and went to get silverware for both of them. "It looks like we'll be eating in the living room since there isn't any room in here for our plates."

She moved past Reggie, wishing he would change the subject but also wanting to ask all the questions she still had. Was it too much to ask him to reveal his childhood with her when it was officially none of her business?

Taking a seat on the couch, she leaned forward and snapped the laptop shut. Resting the plate on her knees, she looked up at Reggie as he came to stand beside her before joining her on the couch. "I don't want to intrude," she spoke simply.

"How about this? If you ask something I don't want to answer; I'll say pass. Then you can move on to your next question." Reggie smiled playfully.

Bethany hated the idea of changing his good mood by bringing up obviously painful stories. "Okay. Tell me about the cabin."

"It was my grandparents."

"I already knew that. What's so special about it?"

Reggie picked at his food with the tines of the fork, stabbing a few noodles before he answered, "I used to spend a lot of time with my grandparents while they were at the cabin. My parents didn't have time for me."

"Okay, that makes sense. You said the cabin was lost in a flood. When was that?"

"Back when I was ten."

"That's when we were in the fifth grade." She glanced at him thoughtfully.

"Yes. My grandparents were in the cabin when the floodwaters washed it away. Only grandma's body was recovered."

"Oh, Reggie! I'm so sorry!"

"Yeah, it really hurt," he swiftly added, raising the fork and taking a bite of food.

Bethany wished she had let the subject drop. Rather than continue, she applied herself single-mindedly to eating her own food. So busy were her thoughts, she hardly even tasted the meal. She had no idea how much pain Reggie must have been in when his grandparents had died.

That was about the same time the incident had happened at school. Why had she been so nasty about the kiss? Well, to be completely honest, Ingrid had been the instigator of it all. Yet, she had remained silent as her friends mercilessly teased Reggie about the kiss.

How come she hadn't noticed him shutting down back then? Could she really have been that oblivious? Kids were so mean, and she had let it happen to someone she cared about simply because she had been embarrassed at getting caught.

The silence stretched out between them until it could almost be felt resting on their shoulders. "I'm sorry," Bethany whispered, her eyes locking on his as he turned to see her.

"It was hardly your fault."

"No, I mean about going along with Ingrid and my other friends."

"Who's Ingrid?" Reggie frowned as he tried to follow along with her thoughts.

"She was the one who started getting everyone to taunt you. If I would've known about what you were going through, I would've—"

Interrupting rudely, Reggie said, "We can't change the past, only the future. Let's just forget about it and move on from here."

"I like that idea. A fresh start then."

"Yes." Reggie looked over at the coffee table before turning back to her and saying, "If I had a drink, I'd toast to that resolution."

"Oh, let me get a bottle of wine. I've been saving one for a special occasion." Bethany jumped up from the couch, eager to put some space between them while she gathered her thoughts about what Reggie was suggesting. Could he actually be wanting to start things over between them? Or was he simply saying it was water under the bridge and beneath his notice?

Juggling the bottle, opener, and two glasses, she almost made it back to the couch before dropping the opener into Reggie's food. "I'm so sorry," she rushed to set the items down onto the table.

Using his thumb and index finger, he pulled the corkscrew out of his pasta and smiled as he held it up. "Do you want me to do the honors?"

"Please, if you don't mind. I'm sorry, Reggie. I'm such a klutz sometimes. Let me get a napkin for you." She rushed out of the room again, her cheeks flaming red. How come it could not have simply fallen to the floor? What were the odds of it landing in his food?

One hundred percent, apparently, she chided herself.

Grabbing the whole roll of paper towels, she rushed back to the living room. Even though she was only gone for a few seconds, Reggie had uncorked the bottle and poured one goblet of the fruity-scented wine.

"This is a good year," he added, holding the bottle up to read the label.

"I know." She took the offered glass and dropped the roll of towels down onto the coffee table. She waited until he had poured his glass as she returned to her seat beside him.

"To a new beginning," he intoned, tapping the edge of his glass against hers.

The small ting of the joining rang out into the silence, echoing inside her head as she raised the glass to her lips. Her gaze locked onto his, seeing his interest in her clearly displayed. Unless she was sadly mistaken, he wanted her, even against all the odds.

Rather than taking a dainty sip and appreciating the vintage, she drank the entire glass in one large gulp. Maybe he had the right idea about getting drunk, so he could face their future. What was she thinking? This was only a toast to a fresh start; he was hardly proposing marriage. What was wrong with her?

"Did you even taste that?" Reggie asked, chuckling at her actions.

"Not really. I should probably get a refill," she said, reaching out for the bottle.

Reggie beat her to it, his hand brushing against hers on the way. "Are you okay, Beth?"

There it was again. He hadn't used that name for her since the fifth grade. She wanted to hide in shame at all the wasted years and horrid thoughts she had harbored against him.

"I'm fine," she said, her voice cracking uncertainly. Clearing her throat, she said, "We should talk about the auction."

"Okay, if that's what you want. I hired the event planners today. They're the best in New York City. I think we should plan a trip over there to go over the details in person."

"Sounds good," Bethany answered absently, her mind going over the details of planning such a long trip across the country. "I'll have to check the availability of flights."

"Don't worry about it. We'll take my private jet."

"Of course, we will," she drolled.

"What? You can't possibly want to take a commercial plane and waste all that time waiting in lines and for schedules.

Nope. As you so aptly put it, we don't have any time to waste on such things."

Holding up her hands in surrender, she splashed some of her new wine onto her shirt and pants. "Wow. This just keeps getting better!"

"At least things are never dull around you," Reggie chuckled. He grabbed the paper towels and tore several off to hand to her. "I'd do the honors, but I'm afraid you might start screaming bloody murder if I came near you again."

Grabbing the towels, she narrowed her eyes accusingly at him. "Very funny, mister." With more force than necessary, she blotted at the wet spots, even though it was rather futile.

CHAPTER 12

BETHANY

"I can't believe how bad the evening started, Shannon. It was so embarrassing," she finished. Looking up from her cup of coffee, she realized how quiet Shannon had been throughout her explanation of her evening with Reggie. Only then did she see the barely suppressed smile on her face. "What?"

As if that question were invitation enough, she burst out laughing. "That's the funniest thing I've ever heard. You really dropped the wine opener into his food?"

"Ugh! Don't remind me." She sighed, setting her cup down on the café table. "I think I really blew it with him. I was such a dork. It's no wonder I haven't heard from him since."

"Did you at least give him your phone number?" Shannon teased. Seeing Bethany's eyes widen in shock, she asked, "You did give it to him, didn't you?"

"No. I totally forgot. I'm so stupid."

"I can fix this. If you want me to, that is. Do you want me to share your cell number with him when I get back to work?"

"Could you?" Bethany leaned forward against the table, her desperation at fixing this situation more than palpable.

Fully laughing now, Shannon simply nodded as she tipped her head back with her mirth. Only then did her gaze fall onto the wall clock inside the restaurant. "Oops. I've got to hustle back to work. It was good seeing you again. We'll have to get together again soon."

"Definitely. Oh, hey! Do you have Reggie's number? Maybe I should just call him myself and apologize for the other night."

"Sure thing." She hastily dug in her purse for a pen and one of her business cards. Flipping it over, she scribbled out Reggie's cell number before handing it to Bethany. "I'm sure he'll be thrilled to hear from you. He's actually been pretty busy getting things buttoned up with his business. He has that huge party at his house this weekend which he scheduled before he found out about the auction. Once that's over, he's turning everything over to Adam. I imagine you'll start begging me to find things to occupy his time when he devotes every waking minute to your project."

"It's not *my* project," Bethany denied instantly.

Waving her hand in dismissal, she hastily turned it into a wave as she scooted out the door. Bethany watched her rush past the window at a fast walk. Sighing, she decided to go ahead and order a bagel since she had skipped breakfast before meeting with Shannon.

Holding up her hand, she caught the attention of the waiter. Once he took her food order along with a refill on her coffee, she sat back and began relaxing. Her gaze kept falling on the ten digits printed out in Shannon's perfect penmanship. Should she call him right now or wait until this evening? After all, Shannon said he was super busy at work. Without any resistance at all, she opted for waiting until later.

The conversation of another patron behind her caught her attention. It was not so much the voice since she was certain he was unfamiliar to her, but more the claim of the man that he worked for Reggie. She leaned back, intent on hearing more.

"When this deal's over, I'm going to be profiting over fifty million dollars. Do you know the best part? He's finally permitting me to head the whole thing. That means no oversight, no interference, and no problems on my part. I feel like I just won the lottery." The man chuckled before picking up his croissant and ripping a chunk off to shove in his mouth.

Bethany had turned slightly, hoping to get a glimpse of who this person might be, but his chair was angled enough to make it impossible to identify him. The only details she could see were his hair color and the fact that he was clean-shaven. It seemed strange that any employee could possibly make so much money on any one deal. Perhaps Reggie's company was more profitable than even she imagined.

The waiter returned to her table, dropping off her food and drink. Because of the distraction, she missed the next part of the conversation. Leaning back with her mug resting between her two palms, she only discovered the men had moved on to planning vacation destinations.

"Charlotte still thinks I'm planning on proposing to her," the same man spoke, his tone dripping with sarcasm. "I wouldn't dream of marrying her. She's only after money and prestige."

"Yeah, but she's totally hot. I wouldn't mind having her as arm candy," the other guy added.

The two of them laughed. Bethany could no longer stand to listen to their crass opinions of the woman. As far as she was concerned, neither one of them deserved any lady in their lives.

She decided to vacate her seat in favor of moving to the outdoor tables. It would be nicer to have fresh air and sunshine, along with peace and quiet. Well, as quiet as a busy city could be in the middle of summer.

Just as she took her new seat, her cell phone pinged with a new email message. Setting down her food, she fished her phone out of her purse and opened the email. A silly grin spread across her face as she realized it was a message from Reggie.

"Beth, I'm sorry I've been out of touch. Busy times here at work getting this weekend's business handled. I've scheduled the jet for Monday morning at 8:30 am. Hope that works for you. R."

Her heart raced just at the idea of Reggie typing out this message for her. At first, she thought Shannon must have put him up to it, but then she realized her friend would not have had time to return to the office before this message arrived. No, this was all Reggie's idea.

And he had been thinking about her. Well, he had been planning their trip to New York City anyway. Still, she was going to have her first-ever ride in a private jet. That was something exciting to look forward to as well.

Then reality hit her. She had nothing to wear in the Big Apple. Those people were used to high fashion. She was going to have to go shopping in the next couple of days if she was going to get everything she needed for the trip.

Her mind raced through the different venues they would be attending. A groan escaped her lips at the enormity of it all. As if it were not bad enough with the tight deadline for the auction, her personal timeline for procuring objects to auction just got shorter. There was no way she could work on the procurement while she was traveling or speaking with the event planning team.

"Ugh," she groaned. Only then did she recall how she wanted to figure out who the man in the restaurant had been. Unfortunately, when she looked inside, the table where he had been seated was now empty and cleared of any evidence of a former patron.

Looking around, she realized she had been so preoccupied with looking at her phone; she had missed him leaving entirely. Shaking her head in dismay at how scattered she had become of late, she decided to kick herself into gear. It was time to get organized. She had a lot of work to get done.

REGGIE

Reggie felt like cursing. Every time he thought he was making progress on clearing his schedule, it seemed like two more items of absolute priority popped up to replace it. At this rate, he would never be able to see Bethany anytime soon. With her fresh on his mind, not that she ever really left it these days, he picked up his cell phone. Selecting his pilot's contact, he swiftly arranged for the flight to be scheduled for Monday to New York City.

Just thinking about being alone with her, even for their relatively short trip, caused him to want to yell out with joy. Of course, being the head of a huge business kept him firmly seated in his chair. It would not do to seem too young for the position and all of its responsibilities.

Just this once, he thought it would be something to walk away from all of it. Maybe he could take his trust fund and have that dream cabin built beside some remote lake somewhere where no cell service existed.

Only if Bethany can be with me, he thought suddenly, surprising himself into admitting his feelings for her were turning into something rather serious. Where his initial reaction was to test the waters with her, he now realized he wanted much more with her. Never would he have taken a bet that she would be a part of his future, yet that was exactly what his mind was proposing to him at this very moment.

"Hey, Reggie?" Shannon called across his office.

He looked up guiltily, wondering how long she had stood there watching him space out. "What's up?"

"I just met with Bethany for my morning break. She asked for your cell number, and I gave it to her."

"Great. That's perfect, actually. I just sent her an email about our trip to New York."

Shannon nodded and then grinned in anticipation.

"What're you thinking?"

"Only that I'm certain Bethany will be calling me to go shopping for the trip. I can't wait!"

"Why would she need to go shopping?"

"Ugh! You men don't know anything!" Shannon clucked her tongue at his ignorance.

"Well, why don't you enlighten me?"

Tapping her toe impatiently, she cocked her head to the side as if considering what to share. "Okay, I'll do my best." She strode forward and took a seat across from his desk. Leaning forward, she said, "Bethany never really had any occasion to dress up. Pete liked her to stay at home, so she never had any real need."

"Okay. And?"

Another sigh escaped her lips. "And now you're proposing she take a trip to one of the fashion capitals of the world. Of course, she's going to need to get some outfits if she's going to fit in. That's where I come in. I'm her fashion advisor."

"Self-proclaimed, I'm sure."

"Of course." Shannon grinned with pleasure.

An inspired thought struck Reggie. Jumping up from his chair, he managed to startle Shannon.

"What're you doing?"

"I'm going to make things easier."

"By doing what, exactly?"

Pulling a black credit card out of his wallet, he tossed it across his desk. "Take my card and buy Bethany anything and everything she even glances at. I don't want her to feel like the price is an obstacle."

Shannon's face lit up with childish glee. It looked as though he had just offered her a pass into the Chocolate Factory. She picked up the black credit card and cradled it admiringly into her palm.

"This is going to be the best trip ever!"

"One thing," Reggie added, interrupting Shannon from leaving his office.

"What's that?"

"Don't tell Bethany what we're doing. Just tell the clerks at each store to pack up the items and have them delivered to Bethany's house by special couriers. I want her to have everything well before she has to even worry about it."

"You know she'll figure out it was you. Right?"

"Probably. But that doesn't mean I need to broadcast my plan." Reggie shoved his hands into his pants pockets, turning his back on Shannon leaving his office. Even though he faced his window, his eyes never even registered the vast view in front of him. His mind created a vision of how Bethany would react to the treasures being unloaded into her house.

CHAPTER 13

BETHANY

Still of two minds regarding the piles of clothing and shoes in her living room, she decided to let the matter go for now. On the one hand, she needed some items for the charity event. On the other hand, she hardly needed to have dozens of options from which to choose.

Just as she thought she might call Reggie out on his extravagance, she recalled the conversation of the man in the café. He was going to be earning a fifty million dollar bonus for his project. Surely, if Reggie's employees were making that kind of money, this pile of clothing was just a drop in the bucket of the wealth at Reggie's disposal.

Not that she did not feel slightly guilty about accepting it. She did. Picking up the designer dress with the gorgeous sparkles, she could not contain the squeal of delight at actually owning the gown. Never in her life did she expect to own anything so fancy. Now she had dozens of outfits that would be perfectly suitable to wear to any meeting or function in New York City.

Her worries on that score were over. Now, she only had to consider what Reggie might want from her in return for his generosity. It went against all of her prior experience with Pete to think that nothing would be expected of her for this kind gesture.

Having received the latest figures on the event planning, she wished she could go over them with Reggie before Monday morning. Glancing over at the clock, she realized Reggie would be fully occupied with his party guests. Shannon had filled her in on all of the details of the business gathering.

Still, she wished she had some excuse to go see Reggie. She could wear this sparkly dress. Then Reggie would see—she shook herself before finishing that thought. "I'm really losing it," she murmured. Still holding the dress up to her, she decided to try it on anyway.

Just as she stood admiring her reflection in the full-length mirror, a knock sounded on her front door. More than a little puzzled, she wondered who could be calling at this hour. She certainly was not expecting anybody.

Slightly apprehensive, she flipped on the porch light and peeked through the side glass. Letting out a sigh of relief, she hastily opened the door and smiled at Shannon. "What're you doing here? I don't think we had any plans, did we?"

"Nope. But what do we have here?" Shannon asked, her tone approving of the outfit as her eyes traveled up and down her body. "That fits you like you modeled for the designer. Are you heading somewhere?"

Feeling her cheeks grow hot, she brushed her hands down her hips self-consciously. "No. It just looked so nice I thought I'd try it on."

Grabbing her arm and hauling her away from the front door, Shannon declared, "We need to get your hair and makeup done before we head out."

"Head out? What're you talking about? I'm staying in for the evening."

"Not when you look that great. We need to show you off a bit. Come on! Where's your sense of adventure? I dare you to come out with me." Shannon held her fists against her waist, leaning forward slightly as she tipped her head in a show of a challenge.

"Fine. But you have to dress up, too. I'd look pretty silly being the only one in a fancy dress."

"Eee! A proper dress-up party. It's been forever since we've done something like this." Shannon dropped to her knees and pawed through the bags of clothing. After discarding several items, she finally stood with a black, skin-tight jumpsuit. "I think this will look pretty fabulous. I always wanted to be a cat woman."

Together, the girls giggled on their way into the bedroom to get ready for their night out. Having Shannon appear at her house was just what she needed to get her mind off of the impending trip. While she looked forward to it, she still felt out of her element with the speed of the planning.

Once both of them were ready, they stood in the middle of the living room, staring at one another. Shannon asked, "Where do you want to go? Out dancing? Drinking? What? Tonight's on me."

Biting her bottom lip, Bethany felt at a loss for deciding anything. Usually, Pete had planned their time together. This was new territory for her. "It's too bad we can't just stay in and eat ice cream out of the carton while we watch a chick flick."

"Oh, no, you don't. There's no way we're squandering all of our efforts looking hot. Nope," Shannon said, rapidly shaking her head in denial of the idea. Reaching out, she pulled on Bethany's arm until they reached the kitchen.

Pointing down, she said, "Grab your purse. We're leaving now before you chicken out."

"I don't know—I have so much work to do." Bethany began pulling back against Shannon's demands.

"All work and no play will make you downright boring. Ooh, I just thought of the perfect plan." She grabbed Bethany's purse without releasing her hold on her friend's arm. "Come on."

Ten minutes later, Shannon found herself in heavy Saturday evening traffic. Her initial idea of going to the dance club was swiftly quashed when they saw the line to get in extending around the block. Instead, she headed back to the freeway and took the first exit to head west. Plan B was on its way.

Another seven minutes later, Shannon exited the freeway without telling Bethany anything of their destination. This was not a part of town with which Bethany was familiar. She turned up the radio when one of her favorite songs by Taylor Swift came on.

So lost was she in her singing, she did not notice where they were headed. When Shannon turned into a gated driveway, she frowned slightly. This looked vaguely familiar. "Where are we?"

"You'll see," Shannon cryptically replied as she began moving forward at the same pace as the gate swinging opening.

Bethany's heart began pounding unnaturally fast against her ribs. She could feel her palms growing damp as her mind began piecing together bits of information. The gated entrance, the tree-lined driveway, then she saw the final piece of the puzzle: the massive fountain in the circular driveway.

Eyes wide in dismay, she rounded on Shannon and hurriedly asked, "Why did you bring us here? We weren't invited! We can't crash Reggie's party."

"That's where you're wrong. I was invited. After all, this is an official business party." Shannon grinned even while she carefully kept her eyes from making contact with Bethany's. She found a parking space near the edge of the lawn, just large enough for her car.

Turning off the engine, she finally shifted in her seat until she faced Bethany. "If you're uncomfortable after we say hello, then we'll leave. Okay?"

"I'm already uncomfortable," Bethany grumbled. Yet her body betrayed her by reaching for the door handle.

"That's more like it," Shannon encouraged when she saw they were getting out of the car. "You're going to have so much fun."

Bethany really doubted Shannon's proclamation. Already, the sound of the music blasting out of the open front door made her wonder how any business could be conducted inside. If they stayed more than a few minutes, she was certain she would have a massive headache she would be nursing until Monday.

Peals of laughter sounded from inside as the music shifted to a softer tune. Bethany had to admit, Reggie knew how to throw a party. Would he be glad to see her? At least he would get to look at one of the outfits he had sent to her house.

Feeling slightly more certain of herself because she knew she looked amazing, her hips swayed more than usual as she walked beside Shannon. The pair would certainly draw attention. Stepping up to the front door and seeing inside, Bethany's confidence flagged as her eyes took in the mass of humanity moving about inside the house.

This was nothing like the calm, quiet meeting she had experienced when she had dinner with Reggie. Her practical nature kicked in as she thought the staff would be spending the next several days cleaning up after this drunken, partying crowd.

"Quit thinking about the housekeeping duties," Shannon admonished, shoving her in the arm.

"How'd you know I was thinking about that?" Bethany's smile betrayed her more than anything.

"I know you. Besides, your eyes kept looking down at the carpets and not at the people inside. We're not going to meet anyone if we stay on the doorstep." Shannon grabbed her hand and hauled her unceremoniously through the entrance.

REGGIE

His eyes must be playing tricks on him. That stunning woman looked almost exactly like Bethany. He missed what Adam said to him as he tried to keep his line of sight with that girl.

"Dude, what's wrong with you?" Adam asked, punching him in the shoulder less than playfully.

Finally paying proper attention, he scowled darkly at his business partner. "I'm right here. What was the punch for?"

"In case you hadn't noticed, Fred decided it'd be more fascinating to speak with the entertainment than to be ignored by you!"

Only upon him pointing out the man's absence did he see they had been left alone. The man was a grade-A bore. He had to find out who that woman was. If it really were Bethany, all the better. "Excuse me," he said to Adam. "I need to check on something."

Grabbing his arm rudely, Adam stopped him from leaving. "I don't think there's anything more important than making Fred happy. Whatever it is can wait."

Rocking back on his heels, he considered how he would reply to Adam. The man was totally out of line. First of all, this was his house. He could do whatever he pleased. Second of all, this was Adam's opportunity to prove himself. How better than right now?

Deciding on the second option, he spoke calmly but with authority, "Then I suggest you'd better make sure he stays happy." Glancing over to the women fawning all over the old man, he added, "I think my entertainment is serving well for now. Why don't you go join them?"

"Fine!" Adam huffed. "But if this deal falls through, don't say I didn't warn you."

Returning the gesture, Reggie grabbed Adam's arm as he tried to shove himself between the crowd pushing in around them. "I put you in charge of this deal, Adam. If it falls through, then you'll find yourself out of a job. How about that for an incentive?"

"You don't have to be so rude about it, Reggie. I know what's at stake here." Pulling his arm free, he pointedly straightened out his shirt before squaring his shoulders and walking away.

Finally free to do what he pleased, Reggie turned back around to face the entrance. Was it too much to hope for that she had stayed put? Finding free spaces to move his way through the crowd toward the other side of the room, his hopes were dashed.

The foyer was empty, yet the door still stood open to let in the cooler night air. Stepping outside, he breathed in deeply, appreciating the fresher air. Just on the edges of his senses, he thought he detected a whiff of apple. A smile tugged at the corners of his mouth as he turned slowly to look back at the way he had come.

"There you are," Shannon announced, stepping from the room he had vacated to stand right in front of him.

"You sure came dressed to party. Are you cat woman?" Reggie lifted his eyebrows in appreciation of her figure. The woman sure knew how to wear black leather.

"Don't get any ideas, boss. Besides, I think my companion will be of more interest to you." Crossing her arms, she tapped her high-heeled foot impatiently. "Although, I think I lost her in that sea of humanity you called a party. Has this gotten out of hand, or is it usually this crazy?"

Reaching up to rub his neck, he wrinkled his nose in distaste. "It's all for the client," he shouted, having to lean in closer to Shannon's ear as the music shifted to a louder tune. "Who'd you bring with you? I could've sworn I saw Bethany."

Just as he finished his statement, the woman of their conversation erupted from the room as if she had been shoved through the crowd. Clearly not as comfortable in high heels as Shannon, she nearly fell as she attempted to gain her unsure footing.

Rushing forward, Reggie caught her up in his arms, pulling her close to his chest. Feeling a sense of déjà vu, he reminded himself not to hold her too tight. The last thing he needed was for her to freak out and begin screaming. Or worse yet, impale him with one of her stilettoes.

Tilting her head up to look at him, Bethany said, "You seem to be making a habit of holding me captive."

"On the contrary. I just saved your life."

"My life, huh?"

"A tad too dramatic?"

Nodding, her smile overtook her face, transforming her into the most stunning woman he had ever seen. Hers was a face he could wake up to every morning.

What? Where'd that come from? he asked himself.

Feeling flustered, he stepped away from her and said the first thing which came to mind. Okay, maybe the second thing. "You look amazing."

"I should. You bought this outfit for me."

"I have no idea what you're talking about. But I like it just the same."

"We should probably get going. We don't want to keep you from your important guests," Bethany said, feeling bad for crashing the party and stealing the attention of the host.

Glancing across the foyer and into the front room, Reggie spotted Adam and Fred cavorting with several scantily-clad women. With a snort of disgust, he answered, "I think the client's having the best time. I doubt he'd even notice my absence."

"Why's that?"

"I don't have the right equipment to keep his interest," he answered cryptically.

Bethany frowned until her eyes followed Reggie's gaze. Her eyes grew wide as understanding fully hit her. "Ah, I see. Well, just the same. I wasn't invited."

"A terrible oversight on my part. Come take a walk outside with me. It's gotten unbearably stuffy inside, and I would appreciate the company."

CHAPTER 14

BETHANY

The heels proved to be too ineffective and downright dangerous once they stepped onto the grass. Rather than risk breaking her ankle before the trip, she opted to stop and take them off. Using Reggie's arm to support her, one by one, she removed the painful contraptions, sighing in relief as the cool grass soothed the hot spots on her pinky toes.

"I still don't understand why women torture themselves with those shoes," Reggie pointed out, shaking his head in wonder at her.

"Because it makes us feel sexy. Don't try to understand. It's a girly thing." Bethany patted his arm condescendingly before removing her hand entirely from him. Rather than continue on that pointless conversation, Bethany started walking again.

"I really do like your dress. The color works perfectly with your eyes."

"My eyes, huh?"

"Among other things we won't talk about."

Giggling, she simply nodded. She liked the idea that Reggie had to behave because of the sheer number of people around them. Granted, it seemed Reggie had led them to a rather secluded area of the yard. She could still hear the music and laughter coming from inside.

"Do you want to sit down by the fountain?"

Thinking he meant the one in the driveway, she shook her head. "I don't want to walk that far."

"No, silly. There's a private pool just over here. Come with me; I'll show you."

Not waiting for her approval, she found her fingers intertwined with his as he pulled her toward the tall hedges. Just when she thought he was going to drag her into the prickly bushes, she noticed a narrow opening where Reggie immediately turned left.

Stepping became slightly more challenging as she suddenly found the fine gravel prickling into the bottoms of her feet. This would not have been a problem if she were still ten years old and used to running barefoot. However, her feet had grown soft over the years, and she had to shift her weight to the outsides of her feet or risk crying out in pain.

Luckily, the bench was only about ten feet from the entrance. The pad which it rested on was a smooth slate stone, providing even more comfort to her abused feet. "Okay, remind me to only wear comfortable shoes here. That was torture!" Bethany declared, sinking onto the bench and leaning over to brush the small, sharp pebbles from her feet.

"I'm so sorry, Beth. I never even thought about this hurting you. Here, let me help," Reggie insisted. He hastily sat next to her and pulled her foot over onto his lap.

His fingers lightly brushed the soles of her feet, feeling so amazing, she felt her scalp begin to tingle. Sighing in ecstasy, she tilted her head back and let Reggie massage one foot and then the other.

This was heaven as far as she was concerned. Pete had refused to ever touch her feet. He insisted feet carried diseases, and he could not be too careful. She shook her head in dismay at how her mind continued to ruin all her good moments with memories of that creep.

"Why're you scowling? Don't you like your feet rubbed?" Reggie's hands stilled, but he did not release his hold on her.

"No. I love it."

"Then tell me what made you sad."

"Ugh. I don't want to ruin this moment."

"It won't ruin anything. You can tell me whatever you want."

"No, you'll just laugh at me."

"I promise not to laugh."

She cocked her head, not believing him for a second.

"Okay, how about this? If I laugh, then I promise I'll lick the whole bottom of your foot."

"Eew, gross. I should say something outlandish just to make you have to." She tried to pull her foot away but found it firmly held between Reggie's hands.

"I've done worse; trust me."

Holding up her hand to stop him from oversharing, she said, "Fine. I was thinking about Pete." The playfulness evaporated from him. She could see the difference in him immediately.

"What about this reminded you of *him*?" he asked, pinching her toes.

She could see he was trying to lighten the mood. Deciding to let him, she answered, "Pete thought feet were disgusting. He refused to touch mine, or his, for that matter."

"What a du—"

"Hey, I never said he was romantic," Bethany interrupted him before he could get fully into his tirade. "What made me frown was how my mind keeps finding reasons to think about him. Well, mostly complain about him. If I'm being honest."

"You're better off without him," Reggie insisted. "If you were my girl, I'd make a point to rub your feet every day. They're perfect, you know. Dainty and proportionate." He looked down and tweaked her middle toe. "Except this one, it's slightly unruly," he teased.

This time Bethany did manage to yank her foot away. "Don't you dare talk bad about that toe. It can't help the way it was made!"

Quick as lightning, he regained his grip on the foot in question. Despite her struggles, he managed to run his fingers along the edge of her toe. He shook his head and clucked his tongue. "You shouldn't blame your toe; this was caused by breakage. That means you're responsible for its deformity. Out with it. What's the story?"

Compressing her lips shut, she shook her head back and forth. She crossed her arms but gave up trying to get him to release her foot. Besides, even while he gripped it tightly around her ankle, he still managed to rub his thumbs up along the arch. If he kept this up, she might just crack.

"I can do this all night. It'll be better for you if you just fess up." He squeezed her heel until she moaned in delight.

"Fine. I broke it attempting to kick a football."

A chuckle escaped his lips. Shaking his head in dismay, he asked, "How did you manage that?"

"Hey, it wasn't my fault."

"It was your foot."

"You know what? This is the dumbest conversation I think I've ever participated in. You've got guests waiting for you."

"I could talk about paint drying with you and be perfectly content. Don't try to change the subject."

"Fine. Nobody told me not to do it barefoot. Besides, I accidentally tripped on the way over to it and drove my toe into a tuft of grass. I kept tumbling, and it didn't. I never even made it to the football. There! Are you happy now?"

"Yes. I can totally see that happening. Especially with you."

"What's that supposed to mean?"

"I was on the football team. Remember?"

"Yes, and I was the cheer captain. What's your point?"

"You were the one to cheer for the defense when it was our offense playing the field. Admit it. You don't know the first thing about football."

Bethany's cheeks flushed. That had been one of her most embarrassing moments. The one moment in her life when the cheer coach had purposely pointed out her mistake in front of the whole team. She never thought she would live it down. Over the years, it became the running joke in the hallways before every game.

"Okay. Well, now that we've digressed back to those awful years, I think it's only fair you share something totally embarrassing of your own. If only to make me not feel so inadequate."

"Hmm. That's a hard request. I don't think I've ever done anything embarrassing."

Bethany hauled off and thumped him in the chest with her fist. "Don't be a jerk. We all have our skeletons. Unfortunately, mine just happened to be in front of most of the town."

Rubbing the spot on his chest where she had tapped him, he admonished, "You should have gone into the martial arts. You pack quite the defensive punch."

"Enough with the defense jokes. No more talking unless it's to share your story."

REGGIE

Reggie opened his mouth to answer when gravel crunching sounded nearby. He hoped it would just be a lost guest who would move on. His wish was not to be granted. Dillon appeared in front of them.

Clearing his throat in apology for the interruption, he said, "You're needed back at the house. It seems there's some sort of trouble with one of the guests. She insists she needs to speak with you, or else she's calling the cops."

"What in the world? Who is it?" Reggie released Bethany's foot and held out his hand to help her up from the bench.

"I'm not sure, but she's starting to upset your special guest."

"Fine. We're on our way back right now." Reggie turned to Bethany and said, "I'm sorry we were interrupted. I'll make it up to you, I promise."

"I'll hold you to that promise. Besides, you owe me a story or two."

"We have an entire plane ride to occupy our time." Then, without waiting for permission, Reggie leaned over and swept Bethany up off her feet. There was no way he was going to let her hurt herself on the rocks again. "Can't be too careful with those toes of yours," he teased.

"Put me down, Reggie. I'm too heavy to be carried. The house is like a football field away." She kept struggling against him.

"Hold still, or you'll put my back out," he ordered, his voice rising to be heard over her vocal protests. Instantly she complied. "That's better. Besides, you're light as a feather."

"Put enough of them together, and they're not light," she groaned, holding onto his shoulders tightly.

He liked how she felt clinging to him. He should have thought about doing this earlier. Not only did he have his hands all over her, but she held him just as tight. He inhaled her scent, wondering if she bathed in apples all the time or if it was just for him. One day, he hoped to find out.

Reaching the front porch, he gently set her down on her feet. Only then did he realize both of her hands were empty. "Where're your shoes?"

A panicked look came over her face. "I must've left them at the bench. Don't worry about me. Go and find out what that woman's problem is. I'll just go back and get my shoes."

"Don't you dare." Reggie grabbed her hand, intent on staying with her until he could resolve this another way. As if in answer to his need, Dillon reappeared at the front door. Practically pouncing on him in his relief, he said, "Dillon, just the man I needed. Bethany has forgotten her shoes back at the fountain. Would you be so kind as to retrieve them for her?"

"My pleasure, sir." Dillon turned to face Bethany, and with a slight bow, he said, "Madam. I'll return before you know it."

"Thank you, Dillon. You're too kind."

"Think nothing of it." Dillon stepped past them and disappeared into the darkness of the night.

A woman's shrieking voice could be heard over the music. Cringing at the volume of it, Reggie turned to Bethany and said, "I should get inside. Will you be okay out here?"

"I'm fine. Don't worry about me. Get inside already." Bethany all but pushed him into the house.

With more than a little reluctance, he left her. More than anything, he wished he had a helicopter to get into with her so they could fly away from the madness at his house. His friend, Randy, had the right idea with a helipad and pilot on standby next to his ranch house.

Just as he stepped through the foyer, Shannon appeared from the crowded room. It appeared all eyes were on the two women inside having a catfight. "You better do something about that."

"Who's the other woman?" Reggie asked, only recognizing one of the models he had hired for the event.

"She's Adam's girlfriend. She decided to surprise him by crashing the party, only to discover him making out with that other girl. If you don't do something quickly, I'm afraid someone might actually get hurt."

"Gah, why can't life ever be simple."

"We're taking off now. Good luck with that." She waved her hand back toward the brawl in progress.

"Thanks!" Again, Reggie wished he could have had a proper goodbye with Bethany. Maybe, once they were alone on the plane, then their time would be uninterrupted. At least he could hope so.

At this point, he wondered what type of twisted game fate was playing on him. It seemed all of their special moments were plagued with problems. He needed to simplify things.

CHAPTER 15

BETHANY

Once again, Reggie managed to surprise her. Just as she was loading up her car to get to the private airport, a Lincoln Town car pulled up beside her. Recognizing the driver, Bethany smiled and put her hands on her hips in dismay.

The driver immediately hopped out of the car and strolled over to her side. He leaned down and took the suitcase from her hand. "I'll take that," he said, lifting it as if it weighed nothing and took it to the back of the Lincoln.

"How come Reggie never said anything about you coming to get me?" she asked, following him to the back of the car.

He merely shrugged and smiled.

It appeared that was the only answer she was going to get. Shaking her head in wonder and barely preventing herself from rolling her eyes, she meekly followed the man to the passenger side door. As he held it open for her, she settled into the back seat and thought about what was going to happen on this special trip.

Special, she mocked herself. *It's a business trip, that's all.*

Yet, she could not keep from grinning at the idea of spending so much time alone with Reggie.

As alone as I can be with event planners all around us, she corrected herself.

The drive to the airport flew by. Before she knew it, the driver parked the car right beside the fancy jet. Bethany felt like a little kid staring into the window of a candy store. Her mouth hung open as she stared out the side window in wonder. Was she really going to fly in that airplane?

Looking down, she noticed a red carpet leading to the stairs of the airplane. That detail made her laugh out loud. Surely, they only did that in the movies. Was Reggie trying to impress her by pulling out all the stops? Well, he had managed to more than impress her.

Not hard, considering my standards are pretty low these days, she scoffed.

The door suddenly opened, causing Bethany to almost fall out since she had been leaning on it. So fascinated had she been by the lavishness of her setting, she had failed to notice the driver coming to let her out. A hand reached forward to catch her.

"Oh!" she exclaimed, ready to thank the driver for rescuing her. As her eyes traveled up the arm of the man, she realized it was none other than Reggie himself. "Where'd you come from?"

"I've been here the whole time. It's too bad the windows were tinted so dark; I would've loved to see your reaction to the airplane."

"I'll be sure to give you a reenactment one day." She wrinkled her nose at his obvious dig at her clumsiness. "So, is this normal?" She gestured to the red carpet.

With furrowed brows, he looked down. It was obvious he had no idea to what she referred. "Um, we are at an airport, even if it is a private one."

"Not the airport, silly. I was talking about the carpet. It seems a bit ostentatious, don't you think?"

Understanding dawned on his face, and he began chuckling. "No, that's standard procedure for private jets. It actually helps to keep the interior cleaner. Totally practical, I assure you."

"Totally," Bethany agreed, her tone sounding uncertain. She wondered if he was just pulling her leg.

Was he serious? Probably, she decided.

Deciding to keep any further comments to herself, she did not want to appear to be completely ignorant of a rich life. After all, her parents owned one of the oldest hotels in the city.

Still, her eyes took in everything around her, liking what she saw. As she stepped up into the cabin of the airplane, a stewardess greeted her.

"Can I take your coat and purse?" Her face was a perfect mask of professionalism. She smiled politely and waited for a response.

Flustered, Bethany began taking off her coat while her purse was still in her hand. The sleeve bunched up and became tangled with her hand, causing her further embarrassment. So much for acting calm, she admonished herself when she finally managed to get rid of the offending items into the hands of the woman.

"It's a good thing you got out of that jacket. By the way you struggled, I thought I might have to step in and rescue you from it." Reggie chuckled as he placed his hand on her lower back to usher her toward the seats in the middle of the cabin. "I like these seats best."

"Oh?" Bethany thought they all looked the same. "What makes these so special?"

"Proximity to everything, but still lots of privacy. Plus, I like the view." Reggie seated himself and looked her up and down appreciatively.

Not catching his meaning, Bethany leaned over and looked out the window. The seats were directly over the wing. She seated herself to see if the view changed at all. With a confused expression, she turned back to Reggie and complained, "All I see is the wing!"

Reggie shook his head as his shoulders began to shake with silent laughter. "You just keep surprising me."

"What did I say?" Bethany reached over and slapped his knee to get him to stop laughing. He should include her in the joke or give it up; anything else was just plain rude.

"You just don't realize when you're being complimented. I don't care about what's outside this airplane. How could I when I've got you seated next to me?" Reggie picked up the glass of ice water the woman just set down on the table in front of him and took a sip.

Knowing her cheeks flamed bright, Bethany had to look away. Turning her body until her shoulders were parallel with the side of the plane, she wished Reggie would quit being so blatant with his compliments. She was not ready for this. After all, hadn't she just decided to make a go of being single to find her true self? Overrated, her mind answered instantly.

Closing her eyes to gather her wits, she slowly turned back to face Reggie. She needed to keep it together, or she would make more of a fool of herself on this trip. Already, she was starting at a disadvantage.

REGGIE

Reggie wondered what she was thinking, her expression staying so somber. He had hoped she would be pleased by the personal driver, the jet, and the idea of being alone with him. Had he only deluded himself? Could she really only want to be with him to get this charity project done?

He hated doubting himself. It seemed to be the only thing he did since Bethany showed back up in his life. Not too long ago, he was blissfully ignorant of what she was doing or where she was in her life. Now his every waking thought was how to impress her.

"Do you like the airplane?" he asked, feeling foolish even as the question came out of his mouth. Since when did he ask such insipid questions?

"Yes, it's stunning, actually."

A little glimmer of light returned to her eyes. He decided to push her further and asked, "Are you ready to hear about my most embarrassing moment?"

A real smile lit up her face. If Reggie could have patted himself on the back without drawing attention, he definitely would have. This was exactly where he needed to go to draw her out of her shell. Unfortunately, he did not have a story readily available, and he had to scramble through his childhood memories to come up with something.

"Well, there was this one time when I was about six. My father was hosting a huge party down at the lake house for all of his employees and important business partners. It wasn't like most of his stuffy parties since everyone was told to bring their spouses and children.

"When I heard about that, I was thrilled. That meant I wouldn't have to dress up in a suit and tie. You can't imagine how undignified those are for a kid."

"Oh, I agree. Totally unnatural!" Bethany agreed, the glint in her eye sparkling more.

"I'm glad you see it my way. I liked playing in the water, and the suit would never have worked."

"Definitely not!"

Reggie chuckled along with her before he continued. "My mother did make me wear jeans rather than my bathing suit. She said we had appearances to uphold, and she didn't want me looking like some orphaned kid out to play."

"That's terrible. I bet the other kids were all wearing bathing suits and swim trunks, right?" Bethany leaned forward, her elbows resting on her knees and her hands holding up her chin.

With her eyes raptly focused on him, he relished her obvious attentiveness. He fervently nodded his agreement to her statement. "Yep. So, I decided to go to my dad to ask him if I could go change. That was my first mistake. I should've just gone into the water dressed as I was. At least that way, I would've avoided all the trouble."

"What trouble? Going to your dad?"

"Sort of. You see, he hated being interrupted when he was discussing business matters with anyone. When I tapped him on the hip, he scowled down at me for daring to intrude. I didn't even have a chance to say anything before he looked me up and down. The next thing he said was, 'Your fly is down.'

"His companions all started laughing, and my father joined in. I was mortified at being made fun of in front of everyone. I didn't care about swimming anymore as I turned and ran away behind the bushes at the edge of the house. I zipped up my pants before sitting down on the dirt in my hiding spot. I spent the rest of the party hiding, too ashamed to go back out there."

"That's terrible."

"Tell me about it."

"I'm surprised you still like throwing parties."

Reggie's reply never happened, as the captain's voice sounded over the speakers letting them know they were getting ready to begin taxiing. The next few minutes became fascinating as Reggie watched Bethany closely. Her hands shook as she fastened her seat belt, and then they moved over to the armrests, where her fingertips grew white with the pressure she applied to them.

He had no idea she would be afraid of flying. It never even occurred to him, given how much flying he had done in his life. His earliest flight had been at seven years old when he was shipped off to boarding school in Switzerland. Of course, that had also been on a private jet with several stewardesses and a governess to watch over him. It had been a great adventure.

He counted her accelerated pulse rate from the artery pulsing in her neck as her gaze avidly watched the scenery rush past the window as the jet gained momentum on the runway before becoming airborne. This was his favorite part, where the ground fell away, and the noise of the wheels disappeared with a final thunk of the landing gear being stowed away.

Within seconds, the airplane slipped between the thin layer of clouds to the perpetual sunshine above everything. He wished he could have been sitting next to Bethany; he would have held her hand to be of comfort to her. Instead, he merely got to watch as her body marginally relaxed as their rapid ascent lessened and they began leveling out for their cruising altitude.

CHAPTER 16

REGGIE

"Do you fly much?" he asked into the silence.

Biting her bottom lip, she turned slowly, her eyes slightly downcast. "My inexperience shows that bad, huh?"

"Only to the experienced traveler," he assured her, an understanding grin forming on his lips. "I flew all the time to get to school while I was young." He shrugged, pretending it was a minor deal when in reality, he wished more than anything that he could have stayed home with his parents.

"Did you like it?"

Reggie wondered how she could see through him so easily. The way she asked the question was definitely aimed at the idea that he wanted more than what he ended up getting. "Most of the time. I just wished things could've been different."

"Don't we all."

The next hour, they talked about various people they remembered from high school and funny anecdotes from their own lives. As he intended, Bethany began to relax and enjoy the flight. Feeling rather cooped up, Reggie unbuckled his seat belt and stood up to stretch his legs out. Once again, he was thankful they had decided to take the larger plane, so he had enough room for his tall frame. He hated the planes where he had to either remain stooped or seated.

"What're you doing?" Bethany called out; her voice edged with alarm and worry. "Don't you have to leave your seatbelt on at all times? What if we experienced turbulence, or whatever?"

"Relax, Beth. We're only required to wear it during takeoff and landing. Of course, it's wise to wear it if the air is bumpy, but it's been as smooth as glass the whole flight. Come on; join me." He held out his hand to her, inviting her to live dangerously.

Truly, he just wanted an excuse to touch her, but he was not about to share that piece of information. He wiggled his fingers, prompting her to make her decision. When he saw her reaching to unbuckle her seatbelt, he withheld his cheer of delight.

As soon as their fingers touched, he felt a spark of electricity. He knew she felt it as well since her hand pulled back slightly before his fingers curled around hers before she could get away from him. Just as he hoped, she trusted him to keep her safe.

"Let me give you the tour. We took off before I could show you around." Bethany looked at him quizzically. "There really is quite a bit to see." He proceeded to show her the lavatory at the back of the plane, the sleeping quarters, the mini kitchen, and the fully stocked bar, as well as a peek inside the cockpit where the two pilots smiled up at her.

"We don't want to distract them," she whispered in alarm. "Don't they need to watch where they're going? I don't want to fall out of the sky to my death!"

Reggie chuckled at her last comment. "Nah, the plane pretty much flies itself. Look," he said, pointing over to the glass panel. "That has our flight plan programmed in and is making all of the necessary corrections to speed and trim to keep us on course. The pilots are here to make sure every component keeps functioning properly. This is all state-of-the-art."

Bethany's expression remained skeptical as she pulled her gaze away from where he directed back up to his face. "I'll just have to take your word for it. Let me guess; you also have your pilot's license."

Reggie snorted at her suggestion and shook his head. "Nah, but I bet I could fly this airplane if I were forced to. I took an interest in aviation out of sheer boredom on all my flights as a kid. My governess thought it was a good idea to learn about it since I was a captive audience anyway."

"I bet she also did it because then she wouldn't have to deal with all your questions during the long flights," Bethany sarcastically replied.

"You don't know how right you are!" He turned to the pilot and asked, "How much longer until we begin our descent?"

"About twenty minutes, sir."

"Thanks." Reggie put his arm around Bethany's waist to turn her back toward their seats. "Did you get enough to eat during lunch? I could have Angela bring us some warm peanuts."

"No, I think I'm fine. That lunch was amazing, though. I don't think I'd have ever thought people ate so well while they were flying."

"Well, you don't if you fly commercially."

"Ah, the royal treatment for the elite crowd, huh?"

"Absolutely! Nothing but the best for my girl." Reggie snapped his mouth shut, wondering how he could have let that slip out so casually.

Bethany laughed, although it sounded slightly forced. "I guess we should take our seats if we're going to be landing soon."

"Nah, we won't be landing for about thirty minutes."

"But I thought he said—"

"That was for the descent. We're at a high enough altitude that it'll take us some time before we're even near the airport to get into the traffic pattern."

"I give up. This is definitely out of my element."

"I could teach you."

"Maybe. Right now, I think I'll just soak in the view from the window." She began walking back toward their initial seats.

Reggie's hand tightened on her waist as he steered her toward the couch near the galley. "Let's sit here together. The view is much nicer without the wing getting in the way."

"Oh, that's great." She seated herself, twisting until her knee cocked up on the cushion so she could get a good view out the window. "It's so far down."

"Yes. I used to imagine this is what the astronauts would see when they were returning to Earth." Reggie casually positioned himself where his hip brushed against her knee.

"True."

They remained at the bench, her gazing avidly out the window, him watching her intently until the sound of the engines changed, and the pitch of the airplane shifted downward. Instantly alarmed, Bethany's gaze hastily shifted over to Reggie's face. "We need to get back to our seats!"

"Nah, we can stay here." Seeing her begin to shake her head in denial, he reached down between them to pull up one half of a seatbelt. "See? We can buckle up right here, and then you can get the best view of our landing." He did not add that he could then hold her hand if she got nervous.

As if she sensed his ulterior motive, she glanced down at his hand still holding the silver buckle. "Are you sure? I mean, I thought we had to be facing forward or something if anything went wrong."

"You sure do worry a lot."

Biting her bottom lip, she took the buckle and twisted around until she found the other half. Snapping it together, she tightened the strap until she could barely move.

It took everything he had to resist the urge to reach over and release her bottom lip from the force of her teeth. He did not want anything to mar her perfect lips. Better yet, he would like to kiss it better after the abuse she put it through.

BETHANY

Knowing he continued to stare at her did manage to distract her from her almost debilitating apprehension of landing. Her internet research on airplane crash statistics had let her know that landings posed the largest percentage of fatalities. She felt her nails biting into the tender flesh of her palm.

The next thing she knew, Reggie pried her fingers open and placed her hand between his warm hands. She had no idea how nice it would be to have someone calm and relaxed next to her. Yet another difference between Reggie and Pete. He would never have thought of holding her hand.

Pete's idea of intimacy was to share a dessert – with two spoons, of course. Too many germs if they were to share the utensil, obviously. Completely unwanted and unbidden, tears began to form on her lower lids. She tried to hide the fact by turning her head toward the window.

Unfortunately, she had belted herself so tightly that she only managed to turn and face Reggie head-on. Instantly alerted to her distress, he lifted one hand up to her cheek and caught the falling tear on his fingertip.

"Hey! What's wrong? Are you okay, Beth?"

His concern, combined with his term of endearment, only caused her to cry harder. She could not force the words to come out of her mouth as she bawled like a baby. The next thing she knew, she had her face buried in his shoulder with his arms wrapped around her.

Her own arms had snaked themselves around his middle, her hands feeling the muscles bunch on his sides as he continued to rub her back in soothing, circular motions. "It's going to be okay. I promise we'll land safely in just a couple of minutes."

Bethany did not have the heart to tell him that his concerns were misplaced. She never thought they would crash; she just felt compelled to be informed of their flight risks. No, she cried for entirely selfish reasons.

She felt sorry for all the time she had wasted on Pete. How could she have thought he was the man of her dreams if he were so selfish? She deserved to have someone who wanted to show her the world and make sure she felt safe in it. What had

Pete ever done to prove that? Nothing! That's what. She had been a fool.

So consumed had she been in her self-indulgent crying, she managed to miss the entire landing. The sudden silence of the engines turning off caused her to pull away from Reggie's now-sodden chest. "I'm sorry for your shirt. You're a mess now."

A true gentleman, Reggie said, "It'll dry. Do you want to tell me what happened just there?"

Closing her eyes against the truth, she wished she could go back in time and remind herself to keep her thoughts far away from Pete. "Just old baggage. Can we leave it at that?"

Reggie's gaze seemed to pierce through her. He must have seen something she needed because, after a few seconds, he nodded. "Come on; it looks like the crew finished clearing the plane. And," he lifted his chin toward the window and added, "our car just pulled up. Are you ready to begin our adventure in the Big Apple?"

CHAPTER 17
REGGIE

When they first met with the event planners, Reggie worried that Bethany would be too shy to get much accomplished. But his fears were soon allayed when they arrived at the venue. To his delight, her face lit up with excitement as she saw the possibilities open to them for their event.

"This place is amazing, Reggie," she gushed again, grabbing onto his arm with her enthusiasm.

He did not even get a chance to reply other than smiling warmly at her before one of the women called her away from him. He loved seeing this side of Bethany. No longer was she feeling uncertain or out of place; she was in her element.

Taking a seat at one of the tables, he took out his phone and made notes on some of the things they had already discussed. So busy had he become with this task that he failed to notice when the planners left, and the room went silent.

"Too busy on your phone to notice the meeting ended?" Bethany asked, her voice dripping with scorn as she seated herself next to him. A sigh of relief escaped her lips as she leaned back against the chair.

"Not at all. I just finished making all the notes of the items we agreed to order." He held out his phone for her to see. Grateful to have been working on the auction project, he was even more pleased to see the look of admiration cross her face as she leaned forward to peer at the screen of his phone.

"And here I thought I was going to get to hold this over your head for the evening. Well, bummer. Good job, though. It looks like you were pretty thorough in your notes. Those guys are really amazing. I'm so glad you found them." Bethany leaned her elbow up onto the table and began rubbing her temple with two fingers.

"Are you okay?"

"Just working on a migraine, I think."

"Good grief; why didn't you say something before? We could have taken a break, gotten something to eat." He turned his wrist to look at his watch, his eyes narrowing as he realized they had been with the event planners for over five hours. "Do you realize how late it is? I bet you're starving!"

Reggie stood up and offered his hand to help Bethany up. She did not seem to notice as she had closed her eyes, trying to keep the light from aggravating her head even more. Having experienced the agony of migraines before, Reggie stepped behind her chair and placed his hands on her shoulders, finding the pressure points to release some of her tension.

His first thought was to give her relief. But he swiftly realized how he liked being able to touch her. If she received any pleasure from it, then they were both winning in this interaction. He would not have to tell her how much it meant to him that she let him help.

Bethany's shoulders relaxed over the next few minutes. A sigh escaped her lips before she leaned forward and rested her head on her folded arms on the table. Reggie adjusted his stance, ignoring the kink he could feel forming on his lower back from the awkward position. If he could help her, then he could endure almost anything. Besides, he had a personal masseuse who could be at his house this evening if he made one simple phone call.

Wanting to make small talk, he asked, "How confident are you that this auction's going to be a success? Now that you've met with the planners, that is."

"Oh," she mumbled, her voice directed toward the surface of the table. "I think we'll be able to pull it off as long as we have enough donations for the auction items. I'm afraid you've had more success with big-ticket items than I have."

"That may be so, but you've got a better handle on the invitation list. Just the fact that you got Taylor to agree to come was nothing short of a miracle." He enjoyed feeling the rumble of her chuckle as she responded to his compliment.

He gave her shoulders a couple more moments of his attention before he pulled away and straightened up as far as his kinked back would allow him. It was probably a good thing Bethany's eyes remained hidden as he scrunched up his nose in pain, valiantly withholding a groan, while his thumbs pushed into the tight knots along his spine.

"Are you okay?" Bethany asked suddenly.

His eyes popped open. She caught him. A nervous chuckle escaped his mouth as he brought his hands away from his back. "Yes, I just got a little cramp." Wanting to change the subject before she started to get too inquisitive, he said, "We should go get some dinner. I hear there're some great pizza places around here. What do you say? Are you up for it?"

"Sounds perfect. Heavenly, actually. Lead the way."

Bethany appeared to be back to normal as she hastily rose to her feet to wait for his next move. At least that made one of us. He figured the walk would probably work out the other aches, so he nodded his agreement and held out his hand for her.

Amazingly without any hesitation, Bethany's fingers curled around his. He was in heaven. This trip was turning out perfectly. He gave her hand a little squeeze for reassurance before they walked out of the banquet hall and into the main lobby of the grand hotel.

As soon as his eyes spotted the exterior windows, he growled in frustration. It was absolutely pouring rain outside. He did not have an umbrella, nor did he have a car arranged for them.

"What's wrong?"

"Didn't you see the weather? We can't walk in that. Here, let me call us a car."

"Don't bother. Look across the way. Isn't that a deli? I don't really care what we eat, and it's close."

"Are you sure?"

"Absolutely."

Reggie grinned at her eagerness. She must have been starving, or else she really was this easy-going. If it were the latter, that would be a first for him. All of the women he had previously dated would have had a hissy fit at the first sign of a raincloud, let alone the torrential downpour actually happening.

Wait! Did I just compare her to my other girlfriends? What am I thinking? She's not my girlfriend, he firmly reminded himself. *But I'd sure like her to be,* his mind added as an afterthought.

BETHANY

Once again, Reggie proved himself quite different from Pete. She would never have expected Pete to rub her shoulders, let alone without having to ask him. Reggie just seemed to know when she needed something and went ahead and got it done. It was quite refreshing.

And disturbing.

How was she supposed to react to Reggie's kindness? Was he expecting something in return? For some reason, she did not seem to shy away from her obvious first answer, and that scared her more than anything. What was wrong with her? Could she not be on her own for more than a few weeks?

Did she really think she needed a man in her life to make it complete?

No. But it sure did make it much less lonely. Her hand still tingled with the warmth of Reggie's hand. Even minutes later, as they sat at the small, dirty table waiting for the waitress to decide to come and take their order, she could feel the tingling across her pinky finger. She had not told Reggie that he held her too tightly, enough so that she lost feeling to her smallest appendage. It was okay; she had clutched him just as hard as they made their mad dash across the street in the rain. Even with such a short distance, they were soaked clean through.

It was no wonder the waitress practically ignored them. They did look rather disheveled and homeless to the casual observer. Bethany chuckled at how wrong of an impression they made. Well, at least Reggie. Here she was, sitting in an almost-empty diner, with a man worth literally billions of dollars.

"What's amusing you?" Reggie lifted a hand to run his fingers through his amazingly sexy, messed-up hair. "Is my hair doing something funny?"

Bethany merely laughed harder at his bemused expression. She shook her head and said, "It's just us. I was laughing at what we must look like."

"Yeah, you do look pretty bad," Reggie agreed dryly.

"What?!" Bethany's shoulders straightened, and her eyebrows lowered dangerously over her narrowing eyes. "You take that back!"

"I was just teasing you. I don't think you could possibly look bad. I've seen you in so many strange situations, so I'd be the best judge."

"Ha. Ha." Bethany bit her lower lip as she rested against the back of the chair. Instantly she popped away from the seat as the pressure of the wooden slats pushed her cold, wet shirt against her. "Oh, that's cold," she said, shivering again.

"This is ridiculous. What's it going to take to get some service over here?" Reggie called out to anyone who cared to listen. His comment earned him a scowl from the two patrons talking with the waitress, but at least she decided it was worth her time to take their order.

"What can I get you?" she drawled, smacking her gum for all she was worth.

Bethany stared unbelievingly up at the unprofessional manner of the woman. If she had been an employee at the hotel, she would have been fired on the spot. Heck, she never would have been hired in the first place. Finally getting past her initial shock, she stammered, "I'd like a hot chocolate and a cup of chicken noodle soup, please."

"We're out of the chicken soup. We still have lentil. Do you want that?"

"No." She barely kept her opinion of lentils to herself. She glanced down at the menu again and said, "I'll take the French dip sandwich."

"We're out of au jus."

Bethany let out an exasperated breath, closed her menu, and folded her hands on top of it. Leaning forward, she kept her gaze firmly on the waitress' as she asked, "What would you recommend for me? I'd like something to help me get warm after running through that rainstorm." She lifted one hand and pointed her thumb toward the window.

"Steak. Cook makes a mean steak."

"Great. I'll take one of those. Thank you for the suggestion."

"Make that two steaks," Reggie added. He picked up both menus and handed them to the awful woman. "And I'll take a coffee when you get the chance."

"You got it," she replied, smacking her gum one last time before she turned to walk away.

Bethany could not help but notice how the woman seemed to exaggerate the sway of her hips as she sauntered along. Yes, sauntered. It was as if she were paid extra for how long she took to put in an order. In that case, she must be making a ton.

"That was quite possibly the worst service I've ever experienced," Bethany whispered, leaning forward so Reggie alone would hear. "She would never last a minute in my family's hotel with that kind of attitude."

Not bothering to hide his disdain, he tipped his head back and laughed loudly enough to draw attention from everyone in the small diner. "That's rich, coming from you!"

"What's that supposed to mean?" Bethany asked, her voice getting dangerously low as she scowled. And there was her proof. Reggie was just like any other man.

"Just that your hotel hires much worse than *her*," he whispered back, jabbing his thumb back toward where the waitress had gone.

"What're you talking about?" Bethany had a sneaking suspicion she knew where he was going with this, but she needed him to say it out loud.

"Like you don't know. It's not like your hotel's *secret* is very secret." Reggie raised one eyebrow in challenge as he leaned back in his chair. Crossing his arms, he practically asked for a fight.

"If my head weren't about to explode from this headache, I'd walk out of here right now."

"Why? Don't like the truth?"

Bethany closed her eyes, pinching the bridge of her nose between her fingers. Taking a deep breath, she exhaled before speaking slowly and distinctly. "What I hate most about having a long family history in our town is the fact that nobody ever forgets past mistakes."

"Yeah, but some things haven't changed. Have they?" Reggie tapped the tabletop to get her attention.

Bethany could not wait to see his smug expression turn to guilt. "I don't want to burst your bubble, but our family has not had any prostitutes working in the hotel for over a hundred years."

"Right. That's why you opened the 'massage spa,'" Reggie said, using air quotes as he spoke. "How stupid do you think we are?"

"Apparently, you're dumber than I gave you credit for. The spa was my idea. Our family business is in trouble, Reggie.

Unless we did something to differentiate ourselves from the competition, we were going to go out of business. Right now, the spa services bring in over seventy percent of our income."

"Yes. Like I said," Reggie started.

"No, you implied we had some sort of service with additional benefits. Frankly, I'm offended you'd even consider the possibility. Is that what you really think?"

Reggie leaned forward against the edge of the table. "Why wouldn't I? I mean, that's been the history of the hotel."

Bethany's eyes grew wide in dismay. "Are you kidding me?" Her voice grew loud enough to draw attention from the other patrons. She no longer cared. "The hotel is perfectly legit. You can have inspectors come any time, day or night. You won't find anything out of line."

"That's what they all say!"

"Ugh! this is exactly why I wish we never stayed in our town!" Bethany covered her eyes with her hand, wishing she could go home and take a hot bath to relax. She would never have imagined the evening turning out like this.

"Where would you go?"

Reggie's soft question caught her attention. She dropped her hand and shook her head in dismay. "I don't know. Georgia, maybe."

Now Reggie chuckled at her. "Why Georgia?"

"My mother's family came from there. They were supposed to be quite wealthy before the Civil War. After that, we don't really know what happened to them or their property."

Reggie stared at her, his eyes practically piercing through her. Bethany could well imagine how he was judging her, just as he had judged her family. "Do you know what I hate most?"

"What's that?" Reggie asked, his tone less than thrilled.

"I hate how your family feels so smug because of how they made their money. We've been busting our butts, earning an honest living with the hotel while yours has been sitting around, loving your Texas tea and feeling all superior about it.

"Just because your land claim happened to have a rich oil field did not make you any better people. Just luckier!"

"Loving our Texas tea?" Reggie asked, a smile tugging at the corners of his mouth. "That's how you think about the industry we've created around the crude oil we've tapped?"

With a tilt of her head, she nodded. "Yes. It's like the British aristocracy and their formal tea parties. Your family acts like they're bluebloods just because of the way they made their money."

Reggie coughed into his hand, his eyes shining with merriment. "I see," he managed.

The waitress finally brought them their order. The awkward silence hovered over them as they set about eating the food while it was still somewhat warm. It appeared the waitress had stalled on bringing them the meal until it had started to grow cold. Still, it was better than nothing.

CHAPTER 18

BETHANY

With the tension between them still rather thick, they boarded the private jet in silence. Rather than take the seat at the bench near the front, Bethany purposely strode down the length of the cabin to take the same seat she had originally occupied on the flight up.

She seethed with indignation that Reggie could believe the horrid rumor that her family's hotel would still employ prostitutes. It had been over a century since that had last happened. When would these people let it fade into the past?

Still without speaking, she fastened her seatbelt and shifted her shoulders until she had a clear view out the window. Immediately, she missed the view the other window afforded. As it stood now, she only saw the wing of the airplane and the landscape in the far-off distance.

Nothing could convince her to change seats now. No, she was stubborn that way. She would suffer with a horrid view rather than give him any satisfaction of moving to a better spot.

She heard him speaking with the captain. Why he felt the need to instruct him in his job was beyond her.

Figures, she thought. *He's meddling in someone else's business. Again! He just can't help himself.*

Her sour thoughts about Reggie were interrupted by a female voice. Confused, Bethany shifted her gaze away from the window to face the stewardess. "I'm sorry. What was that?"

"Can I get you anything before we take off?"

"Oh. Water would be nice. Thank you," Bethany replied automatically. She watched the woman move away, slightly turning as she brushed past Reggie in the narrow aisle. Bethany's eyes briefly alighted on his before she frowned and returned her gaze to the view of the concrete landscape out her window.

"We'll be taking off in about five minutes when the tower has cleared us," Reggie informed her.

She did not think it required a reply, so she kept her counsel. This new side of Reggie disturbed her. Here she had begun to think of him as someone who could be trusted. Someone who was different than the other men she had known. Clearly, she had been mistaken. Reggie was just a richer copy of the typical, judgmental man.

When the plane started to move, she was thankful for the bottle the stewardess had brought her. It gave her something to do with her hands rather than clasp the armrest until her fingers went numb. In any event, the constant crinkling of the plastic caused her to realize how tense flying actually made her feel.

Rather than focus on the speed they began picking up as they barreled their way down the runway, she started thinking about how the sun was getting lower in the sky. She would be able to see the sunset. Her initial thought on this made her laugh. They were going to be traveling into the sunset, so she would still miss it.

Oh well, she thought. *I'll just watch the tops of the clouds.*

"The air is smoother now that it's later in the day," Reggie spoke into the silence.

Bethany nodded, keeping her eyes locked on the view outside her window. She would not give him the satisfaction of making small talk. She might consider it as soon as he apologized for his earlier conversation. Until then, she would remain silent. Let him stew in his own thoughts for a change.

When she was with Pete, she was always the one to break the silence. He held a grudge for a long time, so she had learned to quickly capitulate if she wanted to have any peace. Not this time. She could wait until Reggie saw the error of his ways. Forever, if that's what it took.

The last of the sunlight pierced Reggie's side of the cockpit, flashing bright pink light onto her wall of the cabin. She wished she could turn and see all of its glory, but that would mean having to face Reggie. As it was, she practically felt his gaze drilling a hole into the back of her skull.

No way would she give him that satisfaction. She would enjoy her own view. So consumed had her thoughts been with her frustration against Reggie, she failed to put together the indicators all around her.

Sooner than she would have imagined, the airplane began making its descent. Shaking her head in wonder at how she stewed for so long, she tried to see the lights of the city below them. Surely, something would be out there. After all, they lived in a big city; the skyline should be lit up like a Christmas tree. Yet, all she saw was darkness all around them. Was something wrong? Were they making an emergency landing somewhere?

Glancing ahead of her, she saw the stewardess talking with the co-pilot. They were laughing at some unheard joke. Neither of them seemed in the least concerned about their flight. Maybe it was just later than she realized.

Glancing down at her watch, she saw it was just after eleven. No, not particularly late. She sighed, thinking in just another hour or so, she would be back in her home, drawing that bath she had been thinking of all evening. She could get back to her regular life, one where Reggie was only a person she had to work with for a short while longer on this project.

Once this charity auction was over, she would gladly forget he existed again. At least that was what she tried to convince herself of, not very convincingly.

Through the soles of her feet, she felt the vibrations of the landing gear going down. Still peering outside the windows, she finally saw some lights. Not nearly as many as she expected, but enough to ease her fears of an unplanned landing.

Either she was too occupied with her thoughts, or the crew was faster than they had been before; Bethany was surprised by how swiftly they were told it was time for them to depart. Like a shot, she unbuckled her seatbelt and left her chair. Not wanting to wait for Reggie's permission, she led the way off the plane.

The stewardess smiled at her and said, "Thanks for flying with us. It was a pleasure."

Bethany merely smiled at her and nodded. It had not been a particularly fun flight given the silence they had endured. She turned toward the open hatch and immediately knew something was off. Stepping over to the opening, she came to a complete stop and inhaled the smells of the tropics.

"Reggie, where are we? This isn't home!" she accused, her voice growing louder with alarm.

"No, it's not. Let's get into the car, and I'll explain." He placed his hand on the small of Bethany's back, gently applying pressure to get her to move.

"I'm not stepping a foot off this plane. Take me home, Reggie!" Bethany attempted to back up, only to find a solid wall of Reggie's body behind her. "This is kidnapping! I demand to be taken home!"

"Calm down, Beth. I'm not kidnapping you. And I can't take you home tonight."

"Why?" Bethany turned to face Reggie, her arms crossing over her chest defiantly.

"Because the pilots are only allowed to fly eight hours in a day. No matter what, we'll have to wait until morning before we can go home."

"So get another crew."

"Not happening. There aren't any pilots with the rating for this airplane here on our island."

"Our island?" Bethany echoed, the two words coming out with an incredulous tone.

"Yes. This is my family's island."

"Where exactly are we?"

"Don't worry; we haven't fled the country. Well, not exactly." Reggie put up his hands to stop her from yelling at him. He hastily added, "My family owns a small place in the US Virgin Islands. We can spend the night here and talk about our plans for the next few weeks in the morning."

"As far as I'm concerned, there's nothing further to discuss. We're going home at first light."

"Fine. Can we just get in the car?" Reggie asked.

Bethany wondered at his sudden capitulation. What game was he playing now? She hated feeling like she had no control, and this trip was turning into a disaster. "There better be a bath at this place of yours. I was planning on taking a nice, long one to ease my migraine."

"Definitely. I'll call ahead to make sure it's ready for you when we get there," Reggie agreed, pulling out his phone even as he said the words.

With poor grace, Bethany led the way down the stairs. For someone who only expected a business trip to New York City, this was certainly not on her radar. Taking another deep breath, she rather enjoyed the tropical scents assaulting her. Maybe this would work out better than she hoped. At least she could have one night of paradise before returning to the mundane.

"Wait! Who's going to feed my chickens?" Bethany rounded on Reggie as she reached the door of the sleek, black car waiting for them.

Holding up a finger to have her wait for a second, Reggie finished his call, hung up, and said, "Dillon's already on it."

"Dillon? As in your butler?"

"Who do you think minds my coop when I'm gone?"

Flustered, Bethany shrugged. "I guess I never thought about it." Rather than embarrass herself further, she turned and ducked into the already open door of the car. The dark interior suited her needs perfectly.

Reggie pushed in beside her, forcing her to move to the next seat over rather than being a gentleman and getting in on the other side. "I wanted to apologize for earlier."

"Oh?" Bethany was not going to make this easier on him. She wanted him to admit his mistake.

"Yes. I should've known your family would not get involved in something so—" Reggie paused as he tried to come up with the right phrase.

"I think the word you're looking for is 'illegal.'"

"Yes. I just assumed—"

"You know what they say about that, right?"

"Yes. It certainly spells out how I felt for the whole flight."

"Then why did you wait so long to apologize?"

"Because I can be just as stubborn. Just ask my governess."

"Well, I can already imagine how much you shortened her lifespan if this is any indication of how awful you were as a child."

"Yes. I really am sorry, Beth."

"Thank you." Bethany hated how she melted whenever he used his old nickname for her. He was the only one who ever did, except for Shannon on occasion.

"You're going to like the island. It's very private, and we'll be able to get a lot of work done."

Scoffing, she shifted on the soft leather seat until she faced him fully. "I seriously doubt I'll get to see much of it in the dark. We're only spending the night, Reggie. Remember?"

"How about we discuss it after your bath?" Reggie offered.

Bethany refrained from answering. By then, the chauffeur had shut the passenger door and had seated himself behind the steering wheel. A few seconds later, the car navigated the narrow, paved roads through the lush jungle landscape.

Every now and again, the view opened enough for Bethany to get glimpses of the beaches where the water lapped gently over the sand, glowing whitely in the intense moonlight. She had to admit the setting was rather conducive to relaxation. Since parting ways with Pete, she had had precious little to help her relax.

Still, she hated feeling manipulated into being here. He could have just asked her. Would she have said yes? If she were being honest with herself, she knew she would have refused. This type of spontaneous action was not something she did. It felt reckless and irresponsible. Two things she never associated with herself.

"Besides, I don't have enough, or the right clothes, to stay here for more than a night," she mumbled, mostly to herself as she argued for staying.

"Shannon took care of it all," Reggie put in.

"What?" Bethany turned to face him, wondering what Shannon had to do with any of this.

"I had Shannon pack you a bag. I wanted to make sure you'd have everything you need."

Eyes narrowing dangerously, Bethany's anger rose all over again. "Are you telling me this was your plan all along? You were planning on whisking me away against my will?"

"No. Well, yes. But, I wanted us to have a place where we could plan this event without having any other distractions or obligations. It seemed like the perfect solution. Besides, here we're closer to New York City than back home. We can meet with the event planners practically at a moment's notice."

"So, you've thought of everything, huh?"

With a pleased grin on his face, Reggie answered, "Yes."

"Except for the part where you get my permission. We're not staying here!" Bethany crossed her arms again, turning her back to Reggie as she fumed over his arrogance. She felt doubly betrayed because Shannon had been in on this scheme. How could she have done this behind her back? Could no one be trusted in her life?

CHAPTER 19

BETHANY

True to his word, the bath had been ready for her when they arrived. Bethany's anger still reigned as he showed her to the room she would be using. Rather than try to make any conversation with him, she merely shut the door in his face and stripped her clothes off as she neared the tub.

Within seconds of submerging her body into the fragrant water, she was sound asleep. The sloshing sound of the frigid water around her eventually roused her. With her teeth shivering, she grabbed the plush towel so considerately left within arm's length and wrapped herself in it. Another towel ended up being draped over her shoulders as the ends of her upswept hair had managed to get soaked.

The warm air wafting in from the slatted windows smelled of magnolias or maybe orange blossoms. In any event, the tropical scents soothed her nerves. Making a beeline for the four-poster bed, she dropped her towels and slid in between the satiny sheets as naked as the day she was born.

Uncertain of how long she had been languishing in the bathtub, she never bothered to set the alarm. The sunshine would wake her up in plenty of time to get ready to leave first thing in the morning.

She thought wrong.

The next thing she knew, the sun was high overhead. No shadows occupied her room, and the air stood stagnant outside. Straining to hear any voices or other noises of habitation, Bethany wondered if she had been left utterly alone. "That'd be a nice change," she mumbled, throwing the covers off the bed.

Only then did she recall her nakedness. "Oh!" she cried out. Giggling at her state of undress, she looked around for her suitcase. She spotted a bag just inside her door. Someone must have left it there while she slept.

Feeling self-conscious, she pulled one of the sheets off the bed and kept it around her as she padded barefoot across the cool tiled floor. Wheeling the medium-sized bag back across her room, she once again had a pang of anger at Shannon's duplicity in packing for her.

The least she could have done was warn her. Then she would not have felt so ambushed by the whole thing. "Who am I kidding?" she spoke aloud, unzipping the bag and seeing the light and airy clothes waiting for her inside. "I never would have agreed to this. I still think it's a dumb idea."

She picked up the first items in the bag and hastily put them on. The first order of business was to find something to eat. She was starving, as evidenced by the sudden rumbling of her stomach. "I'm going already," she said, patting her middle.

Opening her bedroom door, she realized she had no idea where the kitchen might be located. Luckily, the strong smell of coffee gave her a clue. Breathing deeply, she headed toward her left, occasionally sniffing the air to be sure she still had the right idea. Within a few seconds, she turned the corner, and her eyes immediately honed in on the pot of dark coffee, practically beaming like a beacon as the sunlight shone down on it.

It must be a sign, she thought with a grin on her face. Her feet moved of their own accord; her mind focused solely on getting the caffeine into her system so her brain would begin to function properly.

"Did you get enough sleep?" Reggie asked.

The voice appearing out of nowhere caused Bethany to jump at least a foot off of the ground. Twisting mid-air, she spotted Reggie sitting at a small table, his back to the window, while his hand held a cup of coffee poised for him to drink. "You scared the daylights out of me! What're you doing lurking in the corner? You're as bad as your servants."

"I don't have any servants. Besides, I'm hardly lurking when I was just sitting here waiting for you to finally decide to grace me with your presence." He tipped his wrist until he could see the face of his watch and added, "It's almost one o'clock."

"No way! Are you serious?" Bethany's eyes widened as she involuntarily stepped closer to Reggie as if for confirmation.

"Yep." He pointed behind her and said, "Get your coffee. There's also some fruit prepared in the refrigerator if you're hungry."

Bethany did as she was told, filling a mug with the strong coffee before she raided the fridge. A few minutes later, she had settled herself at the table across from Reggie. She had meant to scold him for allowing her to sleep so long, but her mind went blank as her eyes caught the view outside. It was simply stunning.

REGGIE

Reggie hardly believed he managed to pull it off. Not only had Bethany agreed to remain on the island, but they had also managed to get along quite nicely. Even now, he watched Bethany work on the computer, her toes digging into the sand as they sat in the beach chairs in the umbrella shade.

He knew this setting would be great for her, but convincing her of the same had been nothing short of miraculous. Besides, he needed to make up for accusing her family's hotel of operating a prostitution ring. He should have known better than that. Of course, his father mentioned it at every turn. There must be a story there, which he probably did not really want to get to the bottom of after all.

The only time their mini-vacation was interrupted was when the event planners told them of a wrinkle in their plans. The disruption to the planned schedule had caused them to actually fly back to New York for one day. Like he had told Bethany, the trip was shorter than it would have been had they returned to Texas.

The auction's plans were coming along nicely. All of the invitations had been sent, and the RSVPs were returning with an amazing turnout. The auction items had all been accounted for, with the bidding guide already printed and distributed to the attendees. The event planners had the decorations and food planned to perfection.

Now, all they had to do was show up in their black-tie attire. Nothing was going to put a damper on their event. He inwardly smiled as he thought about how Bethany would look in the amazing gown she had purchased for the event.

They had decided to dress up for dinner the previous night in their wardrobe for the auction night. When she had entered the room, he thought his heart might burst with pride in how beautiful she looked. As it was, his mouth dropped open, and she rendered him speechless.

"You can close your mouth now," she said, laughing at him as she swept into the room to take her seat at the table.

"You look amazing," he stammered, feeling like a foolish, young schoolboy out on his first date.

"With the amount of money you spent on this dress, I should hope so!"

"It was definitely worth it. I've never spent money any wiser than on that dress."

Bethany held out her foot to display a bejeweled sandal. "Don't forget the shoes. They're positively perfect with this outfit." She tipped her toes one way and then another to let the light catch on the different jewels adorning the straps.

"Absolutely perfect," Reggie agreed, wishing he could reach down and remove the shoe so he could rub her elegant foot. Suddenly coming back to his normal self, he shook his head in wonder. She must have cast some sort of spell on him for him to start thinking about her feet in such a manner.

"What're you thinking?" Bethany asked, shifting her gaze from the computer screen to look over at Reggie.

Reggie felt his cheeks grow hot as he realized he had been daydreaming about her feet. No way was he going to share that with her. Instead, he answered, "I was remembering how beautiful you looked at dinner last night."

"You looked pretty snazzy yourself."

"We make a stunning couple; if I do say so myself."

"Except we're not a couple."

"But we could be." Reggie had not tried to push the issue, but his mind kept returning to his wish to actually call her his own. This new turn of events made him feel uncertain about himself. What if she said no? Would he still be able to pull off the auction with her?

"If you would have asked me even two weeks ago, I would have told you that you must have gotten too much sun in your brain."

"But now?"

"I've enjoyed spending all this time with you, Reggie. You're not like I thought you'd be."

"Which is—?"

"A player. I always saw you with a different girl in high school. Then after school, I thought you hadn't changed since Shannon told me about all your parties."

"Yes. Those were the days," Reggie mused, his eyes scanning the waves breaking out across the small bay where they were enjoying the sea breezes.

"Do you miss it?"

"The big parties?"

"Yes."

"Not in the least. I've never felt as lonely as when all those people showed up and had a great time on my dime."

"Then why did you keep doing it?"

"Honestly?" Reggie shrugged, still gazing out over the water. "I didn't know what else to do."

"And now you're ready to settle down with me as your girlfriend?"

"Well, you don't have to sound so skeptical. I thought I was proving to you how responsible I could be."

"Shirking your duties at the office hardly qualifies."

Reggie jumped up from his beach chair, suddenly angry. "Is that what you think? That I'm shirking my duties? I did this for you. For us."

"I never asked you to."

"I know." Reggie ran his hands through his hair, only stopping when his feet hit the water's edge. Feeling the sand filtering out from under his feet seemed reminiscent of how he felt about how he was handling this situation. Nothing ever went right for him where Bethany was concerned. Was Fate still messing with him?

So focused had he been on berating himself, Reggie did not hear anything from behind him. Suddenly, Bethany's arms snaked around his middle. Her cheek rested against his back. How had this come about?

"I'm sorry, Reggie. That wasn't very nice of me. I'd like to see where things might go between us. I've been wondering for a long time now."

Reggie hardly believed his ears. She was admitting she had feelings for him. Twisting around, he managed to keep her arms around him. He placed his arms over her shoulders to feel her hair blowing against his fingers. "I've waited a lifetime to hear you say those words, and I didn't even get to see your face when you said it."

"Would you like me to repeat myself?" She bit her bottom lip as she looked up at him playfully.

"Yes," he grinned down at her. Yet, he did not wait for her to respond before he lowered his lips down to hers. He tasted the apple lip gloss she had used, and his mind instantly returned to that day on the playground a lifetime ago. This was how they were supposed to be with one another.

He felt her respond to his kiss. What he had planned as a simple meeting of their lips quickly turned into something more passionate. If he did not end it soon, he would do more than he intended with her. The last thing he wanted was to go too fast and scare her away. Possibly forever if he bungled it up too badly.

With every ounce of restraint he could muster, he pulled his lips away from hers. With his hands resting on her cheeks, he sighed and touched his forehead to hers. "That was beautiful."

"I'd say you've improved from the last time we did that."

Reggie chuckled at her reference to their past. "I'd say we both improved." He pulled away from her and held out his hand. "Do you want to go for a walk? The sunset on the other end of the island is spectacular."

"Sounds perfect. Do you think we should put our computers back into the house first, though?"

Reggie shook his head, not willing to let anything practical interfere with his plans for being romantic. "There's nothing here to harm them. Come on. Let's go."

She grasped his hand and smiled up at him with a playful sparkle back in her eyes. This unfettered joy was what he had missed all these years. Finally, he felt complete with the girl of his dreams back in his life.

CHAPTER 20
BETHANY

The cold air blowing in from the hotel's open front doors made Bethany shiver. It only reinforced her memory of the time alone with Reggie on the island. Shaking the hand of another honored guest, Bethany did not have time to dwell on those cherished moments of privacy.

No longer did they have the peace and quiet of the water lapping against the shore. Instead, they had the constant hum of conversation growing louder by the second as more people poured into the event of the year.

Bethany spotted Reggie standing with the auctioneer. He was pointing at the brochure and going over some of the last-minute details with the man. Their original auctioneer had called in sick at the last minute, so this guy only had a few more minutes to familiarize himself with what was coming up.

Watching Reggie smile caused her heart to skip a beat. This man actually wanted to be with her. Was she fooling herself into believing it could actually be real this time? Reggie certainly seemed intent on making her think so. Even as she had this thought, Reggie turned, and their eyes caught one another through the crowd. He raised his eyebrows suggestively as a broad smile transformed his features instantly.

Bethany grinned foolishly back at him. It felt as if they were the only two in the room. For the first time, she wished she could forget this whole evening and just go somewhere alone with Reggie. She wanted to walk along the beach with him, his hand holding hers.

So caught up in her little fantasy had she become, she missed the introduction of the newest guest. "I'm sorry. I didn't catch your name," she apologized. She held out her hand to a devastatingly handsome man. A blush heated her cheeks as the man smiled at her warmly.

"Lincoln Edgewater." He took her hand in both of his, the warmth of his flesh startling.

"Ah, yes. I recall you have an item up for bid. Thank you, Lincoln, for your generous donation." Bethany recovered nicely, all but pulling her hand away as he continued to hold hers for slightly longer than she felt comfortable.

"It's just Link. And it was my pleasure, really."

"And who is this who is so busy with my lady?" Reggie asked, coming over to Bethany's side and placing his arm possessively across her shoulders.

Bethany barely restrained her wince from this public display of testosterone. She had believed Reggie to be above such base actions. She started to say something to that effect when Link laughed and broke the tension himself.

"I'm glad to meet you. May I call you Reggie? I had something in mind for the auction. Do you have a minute where I could go over it with you?" Link gestured for them to go off by themselves, to which Reggie instantly nodded his agreement.

As a parting territorial gesture, Reggie leaned over, making sure to kiss her lips just in case Link had any other ideas about his girl. Bethany playfully pushed him away, not wanting to become a public display of affection at their very posh event. Still, she could not keep the smile from tugging at her lips that Reggie would feel the need to publicly claim her in front of the handsome stranger.

The feeling persisted throughout the evening as different men glanced her way. She recognized the desire in their eyes and felt herself blush more than once at their open admiration. It was nice to feel desirable and wanted again. Pete had made her feel so ordinary. Maybe she really had come into her own after dumping him at the altar.

When the auctioneer finally stood up to the podium, Bethany's heart raced as the main event began. Bethany glanced around, searching for any sign of Reggie in the crowd. Somehow, he had managed to remain elusive despite his towering height.

The guests found their seats and ate their dinner with the music playing softly in the background. Nothing went wrong, and the hired staff performed perfectly during the meal service. She could not be more pleased with everything.

Now avidly watching the crowd, Bethany hoped the guests would be satisfied enough to keep raising their bidding paddles so they would make their financial goal for the Batten research foundation. So much rode on the next couple of hours: the lives of the children affected by Batten disease first and foremost, but also her reputation in the business community. She really did not want to let her parents down. This just had to be successful.

Still not having seen Reggie throughout the evening, Bethany focused her attention on the stage where Link had appeared next to the auctioneer. Apparently, he had decided to include a bonus with his luxury treehouse weekend giveaway. She smiled at his announcement of his attendance with the lucky winner and wondered who would be brazen enough to bid on the package.

Seeing the flutter of women throughout the crowd, she chuckled at Link's brilliant addition. Just as she had hoped, the bidders battled to win the ultimate prize. Link sure knew how to drive up the bids, and she thought about how she could thank him later.

"Mmhmm," she said as the auctioneer called out the final staggering price. "That's awesome!" she cheered to nobody in particular.

"I sure hope you're saving some time for me after the event," Reggie whispered in her ear.

Not expecting him to be there, she jumped forward, jamming her toe into the doorframe next to her. With a scowl of pain, she turned on him and she swatted at his shoulder. "Don't sneak up on me like that!"

"I don't know. It was kind of cute."

Bethany picked up her foot, shaking it a little as she frowned down at it. "More painful than cute," she announced, holding onto his forearm as she balanced on her other foot while she tried to inspect the damage.

"I'll rub that for you later if you like."

"Sounds heavenly, but right now, we've got work to do. It looks like there's only one item left up for bid." She tipped her chin forward so Reggie could see the last item.

"Ah, yes. The painting by Akiane. I rather like it myself."

"Me, too."

"Do you want me to bid on it for you?"

"What? No! That's for someone lucky in the audience." She glanced back over her shoulder and saw the determined look on his face and thought to add, "Promise me you won't do it!"

Wrinkling his nose in disgust, he shrugged and said, "Fine. I'll let you have your way this one time. I'll find something else for you."

"Ugh; I hate to imagine what you'll do next."

"I like surprising you."

"Even worse. Sh. The bidding has begun." She turned away from him, anxious to see what the final total would be for the night. They were so close to their goal.

By the time the bidding ended, Bethany was overjoyed. Not only had they reached their goal, it appeared Link was the person responsible for getting them there. His generous bidding on the painting had done the trick.

When the guests began streaming by to leave or claim their winnings, Bethany searched for Link. She wanted to thank him personally. Her opportunity came when a break in the crowd led a straight line to him. She stepped forward and tapped him on the shoulder.

He looked down at her, his face breaking into a broad grin. "That was a fun evening!"

"I'll say!" She reached over and touched his arm in gratitude as she added, "Thank you so much for being such a wonderful part of our success. This foundation means so much to so many families who have children stricken with Batten disease."

She could not restrain herself from pulling him into an embrace. Her arms went around his waist, and she flushed with embarrassment as he turned and kissed her on the cheek. She had no intention of that happening, but it was nice to have a handsome man want to do so.

With a silly giggle, she pulled away. Her eyes danced with mischief as she looked up at him. "Now, I can't have you flirting with me. It might make that girl you were with jealous."

Link winked at her playfully. The smile tugging at the corner of his mouth told her that he was just messing with her to see her blush. With a final pat on his arm, she said, "Have a great weekend with her. I saw she won the bid."

"I plan on it."

Bethany turned away, her eyes automatically searching the crowd for Reggie. "Where did he get off to?" she mumbled. After all of their weeks of preparation, they had earned an evening of relaxation.

Right after he massages my aching feet, she thought to herself.

REGGIE

Reggie's vision swam with red tinges as his anger almost boiled over. If he had not seen it with his own eyes, he never would have believed it. As the auction ended, he had just finished tying up some loose ends with the financier, and he was going to find Bethany to steal her away.

Yet, just as he spotted her, she was with another man. The man he had seen flirting with her earlier. How could he have been so stupid as to believe she would want to be with him? No sooner had the crowd opened than she was throwing herself into his arms and even kissing him.

The betrayal hurt him more than anything. He thought they had shared so much during their time alone on the island. Granted, they had only shared a few kisses, but he thought they were going somewhere. Clearly, she had other ideas.

He should have known she had a fear of commitment. After all, she had stood Pete up at the altar. Maybe, Pete never cheated on her. Maybe that was just her lame excuse she told people. After what he just witnessed, he certainly believed the tables had been turned.

He stalked over to the edge of the crowd. More than anything, he wanted to punch that smug man's face. His fists balled in anticipation of performing the act.

Suddenly, a woman appeared in front of him. He had never met her before, but she smiled up at him, her eyes dancing playfully with some scheme. He had seen that look before.

Before he could react, she threw herself at him, her arms going around his neck like an octopus clinging to him. She pulled his head forward and planted a kiss directly onto his lips. She smelled of apples. It drove him crazy, and he found himself reacting to her advances.

He had no idea what came over him, other than his anger causing him to do something rather stupid. Still, what did it matter? Bethany certainly did not care about him. Why should he throw away a perfect opportunity to enjoy himself?

The girl abruptly let go of him and stood back a pace or two. "Thank you," she said in a small voice before she turned and ran away.

Reggie watched her go. In a few seconds, a swarm of girls her age surrounded her, laughing and giggling as they walked away. One of them looked back over her shoulder and winked at him.

Realizing he had been part of some betting scheme the young ladies had cooked up, Reggie winked back. His anger at Bethany was only slightly mollified by this strange turn of events. Although it immediately flared again as he spotted Bethany glaring at him from across the room.

He raised his eyebrow cockily and laughed out loud when she turned and left the banquet room in a huff.

Good, he thought to himself. *I hope she liked the show. Maybe now she'll know what it feels like to get played.*

Even though revenge felt sweet at the moment, as soon as she was out of sight, he felt as though someone had sucker-punched him in the gut. He thought things were different with Bethany. Heck, he thought Bethany was different than any other woman he had known. How could he have been so wrong?

Why was it so hard for him to find happiness? Was he truly cursed?

CHAPTER 21

BETHANY

The term 'blind rage' had always sounded so melodramatic to her, yet now she truly understood it. How could Reggie have kissed that girl so brazenly in front of her? It's not like he was even trying to hide it! Even in her anger, she remembered to grab her purse from near the front door as she slammed her way out of the crowded room and into the cold, refreshing air outside.

Her heels made sharp, staccato sounds as they struck the pavement with her long strides. Before she made it to the end of the block, she managed to locate her phone in her purse and pulled it out. Deciding Shannon should be the one to get her out of this mess, given her part in getting her into it, she hit the speed dial button.

"Hey, girl. How'd the auction go?" Shannon asked by way of answering.

"What? Oh, the auction was a great success." Bethany managed to recall.

"Why do you sound angry? Are you walking somewhere?"

"Yes, I left the event right after I caught Reggie sucking face with some chick." Even as the words left her mouth, they left a bitter taste.

"What? Are you sure? I mean, Reggie's totally into you. Besides, I told him I'd hurt him if he did anything to hurt you."

"I don't think it's possible to mistake the satisfied smirk on his face and the wink he tossed my way after he got finished with her. He wasn't even trying to hide it. I mean, there he was in the middle of the room with the girl hanging all over him. I'm not stupid, and I'm not blind. I know a player when I see one.

"I suppose he thinks with all his money; he can do whatever he likes. Just because his employees get fifty million-dollar bonuses doesn't mean he can treat me like trash just because he feels like it."

"Wow. That does sound bad. Where are you right now?"

For the first time, Bethany paused in her walking. She looked around her, confused, and said, "I'm not exactly sure. I just walked away from the venue and kept going."

"Good grief, woman. Don't you have any self-preservation? You can't be wandering the streets of New York at night all by yourself. Do you see any cabs around?"

Bethany bit her bottom lip as Shannon's words rang true in her mind. She was in an unknown city. Alone. Not only had she acted impulsively, but she had also been stupid about her safety. With a cry of relief, she spotted a yellow cab turning the corner and heading in her direction. She threw out her arm and stepped off the curb to make sure he noticed her.

"I'm hailing one right now," she told Shannon as the cab slowed down and stopped right beside her. She opened the door and seated herself in the back. The driver looked at her expectantly, yet her mind went completely blank.

"Where to, lady?"

Shannon must have heard the driver because she instantly said, "Tell him to take you to the airport. JFK. I'm going online to book you a ticket home."

More relieved than she could ever express for her friend's level-headedness, she instructed the cabbie where to go. She let Shannon keep babbling until the car stopped in front of the terminal. After swiping her credit card, she let herself out.

It seemed strange to be taking a flight without any luggage whatsoever, but that was the least of her worries. After all,

Reggie had purchased all of her clothes. Let him deal with them. Just like him, they weren't her problem anymore.

By the time Bethany stepped onto the plane, the battery in her phone was dead. Shannon had stayed on the line with her, listening to her rant over Reggie's actions. It still did not make her feel any better.

For some reason, she had awful luck with cheating men. Was there something about her that forced men into other women's arms? Was she just not good enough? Or was she just picking men who would treat her badly because she lacked confidence in herself?

In any event, it left her feeling terrible. All she wanted to do was go home and shut herself inside until the world stopped demanding anything of her. Maybe she would sell everything and move to another country where nobody knew her, her history, or her family. She needed a fresh start.

The flight landed sooner than she would have thought possible. Maybe it was the fact she had actually managed to fall asleep on the airplane. She never dreamed that would happen to her, but there were a lot of things she never thought would happen which were even worse.

As soon as she cleared the security checkpoint at her home airport, she had no idea where she was supposed to go. Air travel was not something she had ever done before, being too busy with the family business to do any traveling of her own. Just as she fretted over where to go, the sound of her name being called out caught her attention.

Turning, she saw Shannon rushing toward her. A sigh of relief escaped her lips as she hugged her best friend in greeting. "Thank you so much for staying up late to get me."

"Think nothing of it. Now, let's get you home." She looked around before she added, "Traveling light, I see."

"That's what happens when the guy dumps you and your best friend books you a flight home."

Shannon chuckled humorlessly and led the way back to her car. "Now tell me what makes you think Reggie's employees are getting million-dollar bonuses."

"Not just a million. I overheard an employee of Reggie's talking at the café, saying he was spearheading a special project and his bonus was going to be fifty-million dollars. I thought that sounded crazy, but the other guy took him seriously."

"Hmm," Shannon evasively replied.

The drive home took no time at all. Instead of just dropping her off, Shannon shut off the engine and let herself out of the car.

"I'm okay, Shannon. I don't need you to hover over me." Bethany's lips tried to form a lopsided smile but failed miserably. "I'm just going to change my clothes, check on my chickens, and then go to bed."

"Just let me come inside," Shannon insisted.

Bethany thought it strange that she would want to intrude on her so forcefully, but she just did not have the will to fight with her as well. She shrugged and led the way into the house. She left Shannon alone in the living room as she continued through to her bedroom. Scooting out of the tight dress proved more exhausting than she would have imagined, but she prevailed after only one or two seams ripped satisfyingly.

She returned to the living room wearing her favorite sweats. "Are you going to help me feed the chickens as well?" Bethany meant it to be funny, but Shannon's reaction instantly alarmed her. "What's wrong?"

"It's about your chickens. I didn't want to say anything to you while you were on vacation—"

"I wasn't on vacation. I was working. What about my chickens? Shannon, you're scaring me."

"A virus hit your flock. When Dillon came here to feed them during the second week, half of them were already dead."

"Dead? What? No!" Bethany pushed rudely past Shannon, needing to go outside to check on her feathered friends. This could not be happening.

"Bethany! Please!" Shannon called after her.

Not heeding anything she had to say until she could see for herself who was left, she stopped at the fenced area where the chickens usually clucked happily at the ground. There were only two hens left. Feeling sick, she dropped to her knees, her fingers clutching the chicken wire as a cry escaped her lips at the loss.

Shannon's arms wrapped around her as she kneeled next to her.

"Where are the others? Where's Fluffy?"

"They're gone, Bethany. These are the only two to survive. I'm so sorry."

"What else can I lose?" The tears poured from her eyes, making it impossible to even see her two remaining friends in the coop. Her whole world felt like it had crumbled into dust, a barren wasteland of loneliness where she floated without any tethers to happiness.

REGGIE

Reggie dragged himself into the office, intent on burying himself in his work. Nothing could have prepared him for the complete devastation he felt at Bethany's betrayal. He would never have thought she had it in her to be so spiteful.

He should have known when she kept showing up in his life; it only meant she was brewing trouble. Back in school, he had learned first-hand how mean she could be. All of her friends had gone along with her in tormenting him at every turn.

It was no wonder he never wanted to have any commitment with the fairer sex. They played games, and they hurt people in the process. Nope. He was done with trying to find someone to settle down with. While he had professed his hatred of the party life, at least he knew what to expect of the people who showed up. No games there.

If all of this were true, then why was he feeling so terrible? Shouldn't he be thanking his lucky stars he had discovered her duplicity before he found himself standing alone at the altar as Pete had endured? Still, something nagged at him. None of this felt like it was real.

Yet, the fact that Bethany had fallen all over that guy at the auction had certainly been real enough. It had enraged him immediately. Gripping his hair with both hands, he wished he could forget it all, but his heart still wanted to find an escape plan for both of them.

"Well, you totally screwed up this time. Didn't I tell you that I'd make you pay if you hurt my friend?" Shannon demanded, slamming the door behind her as she stalked across his office.

Reggie regarded her as if she were a hunting animal and he was the prey. This was a completely different side to the usually demure secretary. "I fail to see how I hurt Bethany. I think you've got your story mixed up." He shuffled through some papers on his desk to occupy his hands. "You should return to your desk before I fire you for insubordination."

"Ha! Like I'd care. After I'm done speaking my mind to you, I'm quitting. There's no way I can work for you after the stunt you pulled. I'm a better friend to Bethany than you, clearly!"

"The stunt I pulled? What're you talking about?"

By now, Shannon had reached his desk. She leaned her fists down on the surface of the table so her face leveled with his. Her eyes narrowed to angry slits as she spat out, "You deny that you kissed that woman and then winked at Bethany? Really?"

"Oh, that. Yes. I did kiss her—well, she actually kissed me. But that's beside the point."

"Oh, no, Mister. That's exactly my point. Didn't you think that after what Pete did to her, she'd never be able to forgive you for doing the same thing? She's crushed, Reggie. You did that to her. You broke her. Especially after she found out almost all of her chickens died."

"Her chickens? Wait. What are you talking about? I think you should sit down and start from the beginning." He lifted a hand and brushed it through his hair, flattening some of the wild tufts and making himself appear more rakish than before.

"No. I don't have any explaining to do to you. I quit!" Shannon twirled around and stalked back the way she had come.

Reggie jumped up and raced around his desk, beating her to the door. With his hand firmly holding it shut, he shook his head and said, "I've had enough games to last me a lifetime. Sit down right now and start talking. You're not going anywhere until I get the full story. Start to finish this time; no jumping around. My head is already fit to burst."

CHAPTER 22

BETHANY

Shannon had told her she was going to come over. It still hurt to think about her time alone with Reggie. She liked being alone with her two remaining hens; they brought her solace like they had all endured a life-or-death ordeal together. Seated on the porch step, she held one hen on her lap while the other pecked mindlessly in the flowerbed next to the stairs.

Long ago, when she only had one hen, she used to let her have the run of the yard. When her flock had grown too large, it became necessary to keep them penned in the coop or risk losing them to the predators or the cars on the road. Now, she realized she could have the same intimate relationship with her two ladies.

She heard the car pull up out front, but she did not bother looking over. The last thing she needed to see was the pity in Shannon's eyes. It was bad enough that she insisted on coming over and bringing her dinner, but she guessed she needed to eat at some point.

Shannon was taking her sweet time to come up the walkway. Just as she glanced that way, she saw a pair of man's boots. More than a little alarmed, Bethany's gaze shot up the legs and torso to discover none other than Reggie invading her personal sanctuary.

"You! What're you doing here?" she shot out, her hands clutching the hen closer to her middle. The animal began to panic and pecked painfully at her hand. Rather than risk injuring herself or her friend, she let the hen go and stood to face off with Reggie.

"I brought you a peace offering," Reggie said, his voice quiet and gentle.

"Too little, too late. Just leave before I call the cops." Bethany's foot found the step behind her, getting herself prepared to turn and run. Her heart beat wildly in her chest. Why would she still feel something for him other than anger? Was she totally broken after all? Did she crave the pain of heartache?

"Please hear me out," Reggie insisted. He stopped directly in front of her, his gaze lowering to the box carrier he held carefully. He held it out for her and said, "Please take this. If nothing else, I wanted you to have these."

"What is it?" Bethany leaned forward; her curiosity perked when she could hear scrabbling sounds coming from inside. Whatever it was, it was alive. Her hand stretched forth of its own accord until her fingers brushed against his. Just like she knew it would happen, she felt the electricity still very much alive between them.

She took the box swiftly and brought it closer so she could open it and peer inside. Two fluffy heads turned upward to regard the opening. "What are they?"

"Those're Silkies. You can think of them as the alpacas of the chicken world. When I saw them, they reminded me of your Fluffy. I know he can't be replaced, but I hoped these two would make you smile when you saw them."

"I can certainly see their resemblance to an alpaca – all that fluff is ridiculous. They're adorable; that's for sure." Then, for no reason, she burst into tears. Reggie could be so kind and thoughtful, these chickens just proved it, but then he had hurt her so badly. How could she trust him? Why would her heart keep turning to him when she knew it could not work between them?

Reggie's arms went around her, further confusing her already bruised heart. She wanted to melt into him, let him comfort her, and tell her everything would be okay. She needed a moment alone to think things through.

Pulling away, she used the only excuse she could come up with on the spot. "I bet they're thirsty." She brushed past Reggie on her way back to the chicken coop. The two hens followed her faithfully, hoping for some treats to be disbursed.

REGGIE

Reggie felt like a nickel as soon as he saw how terrible Bethany looked on her porch. It was as if all of the light had been pulled out of her. She used to shine and sparkle just by walking into a room.

He had done this to her. He had to make it better. At least the Silkie chickens had made her smile a little. He wished that smile had been directed at him, but he was willing to take any win at this point.

Following her to the chicken pen, he wished he had a better way to apologize than the lame lines he had thought up in the car on the drive over. Deciding to head right to the heart of the matter, he stated, "Shannon told me I made a total mess of everything with you."

"I'd say she was right."

"But I thought you were playing me."

"How?" Bethany turned and looked over at him incredulously. "What would ever give you that impression?"

"The way you threw yourself at that guy at the auction. What was I supposed to think about that? I saw the two of you kissing and so—"

"I didn't kiss anyone at the auction. Are you drunk, Reggie?"

"Perfectly stone-cold sober, unfortunately. I know what I saw." Yet, as he saw her open denial of what he had believed to be facts, he realized something was definitely wrong with his initial take on the situation.

Had he really been so insecure with Bethany that he had invented a scenario where they couldn't be together? Had he done this to himself and managed to hurt Bethany in the process? One thing was certain; they needed to talk this through.

Bethany turned and crossed her arms defensively across her chest. "Well, I think I'd know if I kissed anyone. What I do recall, very clearly, is seeing you making out with that girl in the corner and then flaunting it to me. Try to deny that!"

"That was nothing!" His heart sank at how terribly he had handled that stupid girl's kiss. Even then, he knew the girl had used him to win a bet with her friends, but he had used her game to hurt Bethany. How stupid and immature could he be?

"Says the guy who enjoyed it! I don't want to hear anything more about this, Reggie. You're not worth my time."

She made to walk past him, but Reggie's arm shot out and held her captive in front of him. He needed her to listen to him. There was no way he was going to let another childish misunderstanding take her away from him.

"I'd let go if I were you," she spoke with deadly calm.

"Not until you hear me out." All his life, she had felt like the one he was supposed to be with. Today, he needed to make her see that as well.

They both knew this position felt oddly familiar.

BETHANY

By the time they both heard the actual stories of the other, they realized how big of a mistake they had made. With the truth laid out so plainly between them, they threw their arms around one another and hugged as if their lives depended on it.

"Can we make a pact to never go through anything like this again?" Bethany asked, her voice muffled in the folds of his shirt. He barely gave her any room to breathe, and she would not have it any other way.

She had to let go of her distrust; Reggie did not deserve it. They both had baggage from their pasts, but they could work through it as long as they talked things through. Her heart had always been his; Pete had merely been a distraction from her truth.

"Absolutely. As long as you can agree, you'll never even speak to another man unless I'm present."

"I'm not agreeing to that, Reggie." She knew he was only joking with her now and smiled playfully up at him. They had turned the corner in their relationship. While she had grown to love him during their time on the island, she had not learned to trust him completely until now.

"Hey, a guy can hope. But seriously, I'm so sorry for thinking you were capable of—I don't even want to say it. I feel so stupid."

"You are stupid. That's why we mesh so well. We're both stupid."

"I think as long as I have you, then I'll be able to heal."

"I think we've already come a long way just today. There's been so much pain in us not being together. And I don't mean just these last few weeks. This drama has been brewing for over fifteen years. We can't keep allowing this to happen."

"Definitely not." Reggie pulled her away from him and held out his pinky toward her. "I pinky promise to always tell you when I feel frustrated. And I promise to listen to your side of the story, even if I think I already know what's going on."

Bethany looked down at his hand, his pinky poised and ready for her to link with her own. It seemed so silly for him to remember this promise. They had only been ten when she made him promise always to be hers. They had linked pinkies, just as she did now with him. It felt like it all came full circle, and her eyes filled with tears as she realized she was finally going to have her forever with the only man who had ever stolen her ten-year-old heart.

"I love you, Reggie."

He tipped his head until their foreheads touched. "I love you, Beth. We're going to make an amazing team. We'll be unstoppable."

"Only if I can pry you away from work."

"Well, your little bombshell about Adam certainly made life interesting. I don't know what I would've done had he actually managed to embezzle all the funds he had put together. Do you realize he was only two weeks away from his personal golden parachute?"

"I'm just sorry I didn't say something to Shannon earlier. What's going to happen with him?"

"Oh, he's definitely going to jail. There's no way we can let him get away with such a scheme. Plus, we discovered four other key employees who were complicit with the plan. They're gone too."

"So now what? Are you going to have to work overtime putting the pieces back together?" Bethany's heart sank at the idea of him devoting most of his time to the office. They had just rediscovered one another.

"Definitely not. I promoted Shannon to CEO. She's working with the Board of Directors to get some new management into the company."

"Shannon? Really? What made you think of her for the position?"

"The truth?"

"Always!"

"I discovered just how shrewd she could be when she came and gave me a dressing down for hurting you. I'm not sure I would've ever seen her ruthless side if it weren't for our little escapade in New York."

"Well, at least that awful experience helped someone. I'm glad for her. She deserves it."

"I quite agree. That gives us time to begin dating. We can take things as slowly as you want."

"I don't want slow. As far as I'm concerned, we could elope to Vegas, and that'd be fine by me." Bethany's hand flew up to cover her mouth. "I'm sorry, Reggie. I didn't mean to sound so desperate. It's not like you were proposing or anything. I just jumped the gun a bit."

"I quite like your spontaneous side." Reggie dipped his hand into his jeans pocket and pulled out his cell phone. He wiggled his eyebrows at her as he dialed and brought the phone up to his ear. "Get the plane ready. We're heading to Vegas."

Bethany's eyes grew wide with excitement. "Are you serious?"

"Absolutely. I wouldn't dare dream of joking about this kind of thing. As long as you're not upset about not having the big, fancy wedding with all the family and trimmings."

Bethany shook her head in adamant denial. "No way! I mean, I've already tried the traditional wedding route and found it's not my style at all. This is going to be amazing! We need to call Shannon."

"No need," she called out from behind them.

Bethany turned and ran toward her friend. "What're you doing here? How much did you hear?"

"I told you I was coming over, and I've been here long enough to know you two worked everything out. I'm so happy for you. So, do I get to be your Maid of Honor this time?"

"I wouldn't have it any other way!" Bethany hugged her again before turning to face Reggie. A huge grin spread across her face, and her eyes lit up with excitement as a squeal of delight escaped her lips. "This is really happening!"

Reggie closed the distance between them and grabbed her up into his arms. Without warning, he planted a kiss full on her lips, heedless of their audience. Together they turned in circles until they were both dizzy and laughing at their silliness.

They had so much to look forward to. Together, they would set the world on fire. Nothing would ever come between them again. The pinky promise had sealed the deal.

EPILOGUE

(SIX MONTHS LATER) - BETHANY

Stepping out of the Cadillac Escalade, Bethany looked around in confusion. Never having been to Georgia before, she discovered it was everything she expected. With the exception of the dilapidated house in front of her. "What is this place?" she asked her husband.

Coming to stand beside her, pulling her closer to him with his arm around her shoulders, Reggie grinned down at her and said, "This is your family's plantation."

"What? How on Earth did you find it? We never even had an address; only the stories passed down through the generations." She tore her gaze away from Reggie to look in wonder at this new revelation. This was where her family had landed when they first got off the boat from England. This was her legacy.

"I hired a genealogist to trace your family lineage. It was a simple matter to purchase the property once we discovered its actual location."

"Wait! Did you buy this? I thought you were merely surprising me with the visit. I can't believe you did all this just because of a simple conversation between us months ago." Bethany turned, her mouth hanging open in wonder.

"It's all yours now, baby. Purchased in your name alone. I want this to be your special place. Once we hire a construction crew, you can design everything inside the house to be exactly as it was. Or, if you want to demolish everything and start over, you can do that too."

"No way! This house is beautiful just the way it is!" Bethany moved away from Reggie to step closer to the house. Seeing the porch steps sagging in disrepair and the siding all but falling off, she chuckled before adding, "Okay, maybe it could use a little help."

"Thank goodness! I thought you might get the idea in your head of keeping it looking like the house from the Amityville Horror."

Swatting playfully at his arm, she shook her head as she suppressed her laughter. "Don't even joke about that. I'm already paranoid enough without you giving me any more ideas." She placed her hand in his and pulled him around to the side of the house. Now that she knew this place was hers, she wanted to see it all. "How many acres come with the house? I'm sure it's nothing compared to what the original deed had, but that's okay."

"I told you I bought the original deed. All ten thousand acres. Your legacy is intact again, safe for future generations of Bartholomew's."

"I like the sound of that!" Shaking her head in wonder, she stepped in front of Reggie and pulled his head down close to hers. "I don't know what I did to deserve you, but I sure am glad we took another chance with each other." She pressed her lips against his, feeling him respond to her touch instantly. It never ceased to amaze her how perfect they were together. How could she have let him go? Never again. No more wasted time.

After a few minutes of being lost in one another's touch, the sound of someone clearing their throat interrupted them. Bethany pulled away, wiping her bottom lip as she turned to see who had appeared. Recognizing him immediately as one of Reggie's best friends, who also happened to be a real estate agent, she grinned and said, "I suppose you had something to do with this surprise, huh, Michael?"

"Absolutely. I'm a sucker for romantic gestures," Michael agreed, stepping forward to clap Reggie on the back of his shoulder. "Looks like someone's getting lucky tonight!"

Scoffing at his friend's crass joke, Reggie smiled as he shook his head in dismay. "Why don't you make yourself useful and share what you found out about this property?" He held out his hand for Bethany to entwine her fingers with his as they walked the property with Michael.

"Well, there are sixteen structures on the property. Some of them are pretty shabby, but there's still history in them. There's a lake down the lane over there," he said, pointing off to their left at a path that looked a little better than a game trail.

"Let's go check that out," Bethany urged, tugging slightly on Reggie's hand.

REGGIE

Never in a million years would he tell her the exorbitant price he had paid for the property. Seeing her happiness was payment in full, as far as he was concerned.

They walked single-file down the track. Reggie already planned on bringing some equipment in to widen the access.

When they finally reached the lake, he came to a dead stop to take in the vista view.

Off to his right, a small cabin with a broad, covered front porch sat perched above the edge of the lake. It was almost exactly like his grandparents' cabin. Granted, it had been years since he had last seen it, but his memories came flooding back as he took hesitant steps to bring him closer.

"What's wrong, Reggie?" Bethany asked, her initial excitement for the place dampened with her concern for her husband.

"This place. It's perfect," he whispered, his face lighting up in wonder.

"Does it remind you of your dream to live in a cabin?" She wrapped her fingers around his elbow as she came to stand next to him, her gaze looking over the small wooden structure. "Maybe we could fix this place up first and live here while the big house is being repaired."

"Were you thinking about moving here?" Reggie asked.

"Yes. Weren't you?"

"I guess I never thought about that. I just figured this could be a summer retreat or something."

"Oh no! This place is too special for that. Reggie, just think about it. We can make our own way here. No expectations of anyone except ourselves. Doesn't that sound perfect?"

Hearing the yearning in her voice, Reggie found himself nodding in agreement. "Yes. I think that's the perfect plan." Turning to Michael, Reggie asked, "Do you have any contractor friends who can devote their time to this massive project?"

"I'm sure I can find the perfect crew for you. I'll get on it right away."

"Maybe you can find a lady friend to help you with it while you're at it," Bethany teased.

Michael chuckled without humor. "Nope. Marriage may be perfect for you two and for Randy. I'm content with my career and carefree life. Thank you very much."

"Famous last words," Reggie teased, nudging Michael on the shoulder.

Reggie turned back toward the cabin, deciding to investigate the interior since they were so close. He hoped it would have a sound foundation. Everything else would be easier to fix if that were still okay. Somehow, he knew what he would find inside.

The perfect view from the porch could not have been more exact than the vision he held inside his head all these years. Turning slowly, he could almost feel his grandparents looking down on him. This was his new home, of that he was certain.

Draping his arm around his wife's waist, he said, "Welcome home, my love."

"Thank you, Reggie. This'll be the perfect start for our growing family." She tipped her head until her cheek rested on his shoulder, both of them staring out across the water.

"Wait! Are you saying what I think you are? Are you pregnant?"

"Yes. Are you happy?"

Reggie felt his knees go weak at this revelation. Never before had he considered what it would be like to have his own family. Now, he was going to have everything even beyond his dreams. His life was absolutely perfect. The tears glistened as they fell down his cheeks. With his voice apparently gone, all he could do was nod in affirmation.

The End...For Now

Continue the series with Properties of Love, Book 3, in the Billionaire's Bet Romances.

CHAPTER 23

BONUS: FIRST CHAPTER OF PROPERTIES OF LOVE

Impatience gnawed at Michael like a restless tiger as he stood in the Title company, waiting to get his hands on the all-important land deed documents. He tapped his foot impatiently, but then his gaze fell on the stunning woman working at the desk across from him. Well, that certainly made the wait more tolerable.

When his phone buzzed in his pocket, he was ready to growl in frustration, but his friend's name on the caller ID saved him from any outbursts. Turning away from the captivating woman, Michael leaned against the well-worn counter, phone pressed to his ear.

"They have no idea what's happening in their neighborhood," Michael chuckled, feeling like he was about to spill some top-secret heist. "I've been snapping up these properties at one-tenth of the value I'll have by this time next year."

His friend on the other end was probably shaking his head in disbelief at Michael's lucky streak. Little did he know the hours of research and strategic planning Michael had put into this game. Oh, it was all about to pay off big time.

Michael chuckled at his personal coup, once again lining his ultra-wealthy pockets with unsuspecting people's properties. He didn't see the shabby office around him; instead, he focused on the plans for the construction of a massive mall complex.

His careful research and donations in the right places allowed him the knowledge to always show up in the right place at the right time. He let people believe in his incredible luck, but he knew all of the hours of reading and listening that went into his particular kind of success. So much rode on him making a name for himself.

For years, he had been under his father's watchful eye, working in the family business. But Michael wanted to prove himself, to carve out his own legacy. So, he took a leap of faith, and now he was the king of his real estate empire.

But what amused him the most was how people underestimated him just because he looked young for his twenty-seven years They thought they had the upper hand, and Michael loved watching their smug faces turn to disbelief when he outsmarted them at every turn. He was a real estate ninja, stealthily maneuvering through contracts and negotiations.

But they learned. The tiger was on the prowl, and he was about to make another killing in the real estate jungle. And when he walked away with deals others thought were impossible, he would do it with finesse and class, never once gloating. After all, what's a victory without a little mystery and style?

Despite his privileged upbringing in his father's billion-dollar investment company, family life had been anything but happy. His parents' constant discord drove him away from their opulent mansion and into the arms of his loving grandmother.

Suddenly, the air around him filled with a tantalizing scent of vanilla, signaling the approach of someone he knew all too well. Just as expected, a thick manila envelope landed on the countertop behind him. With a slick smile, Michael swiftly ended his phone call and turned around to face the source of the delightful fragrance.

Jocelyn.

Her shoulder-length blonde hair framed her captivating doe eyes, and Michael couldn't help but admire her beauty. Despite his cheeky demeanor, he felt genuine gratitude for her speedy service. However, the playful glint in his eyes clashed with her stern expression.

"Thanks, Josie. I appreciate the speedy service, as always," he said with a smirk, purposely using the nickname he knew annoyed her.

"It's Jocelyn, Mr. Cavanaugh, but whatever," she retorted, rolling her eyes before making a swift exit.

Her sassy departure only amused him further, and he couldn't help but admire her from behind as she walked away. He loved riling her; she made it so easy.

Maybe he had been going about it all wrong with her. Perhaps instead of riling her up, he should try a different approach. He found himself contemplating the idea of asking her out.

After his last relationship fizzled out a couple of months ago, he had kept to himself, focusing on work and more important pursuits. But just the thought of Jocelyn's full lips against his brought a mischievous glimmer to his eyes. Yes, maybe it was time to soften up the prickly little Jocelyn and see where that might lead. After all, what's life without a little excitement and a lot of charm?

With the hefty packet in hand, Michael couldn't help but admire Jocelyn's meticulous work. Her attention to detail impressed him more than she could ever imagine, and it was the reason he almost exclusively used this shabby, old title company for his business. Loose ends and delays were not something he could tolerate. Any hiccup could jeopardize a deal, and that was simply unacceptable in his world.

Feeling the documents safely tucked under his arm, he had more than business on his mind as he strode out of the bustling office into the sultry heat of the Georgian sun. The idea of winning over Josie occupied his thoughts, and he couldn't help but devise a charming plan.

He paid no attention to the beauty of the flowering hibiscus right in front of his car. If someone dared to ask him about the scenery, they would have received a blank stare. Scenery? Who had time for that? He had deals to close and ventures to conquer.

In the scorching heat, he refused to loosen his tie. Maintaining the image of a cool and composed businessman was crucial, after all. Luckily, he had snagged the prime parking spot near the entrance, allowing him to reach his sleek

Mercedes AMG with ease. As he settled into the luxurious leather seat, he couldn't escape the heat, even with the window cracked open.

The car's interior felt like an oven, and he half-jokingly wondered if he could bake cookies on the dashboard. Despite the sweltering heat, he kept his focus on his next task, his mind buzzing with ideas and strategies.

Tossing the paperwork onto the passenger seat, Michael started the engine with a smooth gesture. The vents immediately blasted hot air into his face, but he knew relief was on the way as the AC kicked in.

With the tunes blaring from the radio, he sped out of the parking lot, squeezing his car into a tight space between two vehicles, earning a honk from the impatient driver behind him. Crazy drivers couldn't deter him; he had places to be and promises to keep.

With five minutes to spare, he pulled into his reserved parking space. As Georgia's most eligible bachelor, he was used to the attention from women, single or married, everywhere he went, but he doggedly ignored the staff's stares. His past experiences had taught him to keep his guard up, protecting himself from getting hurt again.

Navigating through the bright and colorful hallways, he hardly noticed the colorful paintings on the walls, his mind preoccupied with more pressing matters. Finally, he reached the room that held someone dearer to him than anything else in the world. A deep breath steadied him as he prepared for the encounter.

With a light tap on the six-panel wooden door, he turned the shiny, brass handle to let himself in, fully expecting to see a familiar smile greeting him.

But as he entered, he was taken aback. Instead of his grandma, a stranger occupied the room. "Who are you?" Michael blurted out, pushing his way inside to find his beloved grandmother.

His mind spun with dreadful scenarios in the absence of his grandma, none of them offering any comfort. His heart raced like a runaway train, and his eyes darted around the room in panic. Everything in his grandma's room remained undisturbed—the dressers, coffee table, and chairs—yet she was nowhere to be seen.

"Come sit down, Michael. Let me explain why I'm here today," the man said without rising or even introducing himself.

Already suspicious, Michael didn't trust the stranger, resenting the fact that he knew his name without any proper introduction. The man exuded self-assurance, just like his father, and it put him on edge.

Hating to be caught off guard, Michael needed all the facts before making any decisions—this felt like a cold business transaction, and he wanted no part of it, especially if it meant his grandma had passed away.

"I'll stand," Michael replied curtly, feeling the uncomfortable trickle of sweat down his back. His main concern was his grandma's whereabouts, and he demanded, "Where's Evelyn?"

"I'm right here, Mikey. Come help me to my bed." A frail, trembling voice emanated from the doorway leading to the private bathroom. Michael's heart clenched as he saw his grandma's fragile figure, ravaged by the relentless grasp of Parkinson's disease.

Without hesitation, Michael hurried to her side, gently enveloping her in his embrace. Using his height and strength, he supported her, realizing how much more weight she had lost. Concern and fear flooded him as he felt the prominence of her bones through the rich silk fabric of her dressing robe.

Michael couldn't bear to see his grandma's frailty, so he carefully positioned her in the middle of the bed, gently fluffing the pillows behind her delicate frame. He feared that even his touch might be too much for her weakened state.

Biting his bottom lip to suppress his emotions, he stepped back and turned his attention to the stranger in the room. He needed to focus on this man's business to distract himself from the overwhelming worry.

Evelyn arranged the covers just as she liked them and she patted the edge of the bed. Her once strong voice now barely a whisper said, "Mikey, sit next to me and listen to what Mr. Nitro has to say."

Mr. Nitro? What kind of name was that? It sounded phony, just like the smile plastered on the man's pudgy face. Before following his grandma's instruction, Michael muttered, "Mr. Nitro, if that's your real name," and then boldly asked, "Why are you here?"

"Be nice, Mikey. Kevin is my attorney, and he has been for many years," Evelyn chided, her trembling hand reaching for his thigh.

Disliking the feel of her tremors, Michael pressed his hand down gently over hers, trying to offer some comfort. The feeble strength of her hold only made him feel more helpless.

No amount of money could fix the person he loved most in the world. He nodded reluctantly, shifting his gaze back to the unwanted guest.

"I'm here at your grandmother's behest," Kevin said, seeking Evelyn's approval before continuing. Satisfied with her nod, he continued, "It seems Ms. Evelyn has received the results of her latest tests and only has about six months left to live."

His jaw clenched. He despised the fact that this man had such news about his grandma, news that he hadn't been made aware of before.

Tension gripped Michael as he tried to keep his fingers relaxed, not wanting to hurt his grandma with his own fear. He vehemently shook his head in denial, refusing to accept the harsh truth. "I don't believe you. We're going to have them redo the tests."

Turning to his grandma, desperation in his eyes, he hoped she would contradict the attorney's words. But her sad gaze confirmed the dreadful news. "If this place can't take care of your needs properly, then we'll move you to a better facility. Money's no object. I'll start making phone calls right now."

His hand instinctively reached for his phone in his front pocket, but her next words halted him in his tracks.

"You'll do nothing of the kind, Michael."

She only called him by his given name when he was in trouble.

Feeling chastised and embarrassed in front of a stranger, Michael nodded mutely, biting back the sharp retort he wanted to make. "State your business, Mr. Nitro, so that I can have some private time with my grandma." More than ever, he wanted to have these precious moments alone with the woman who had practically raised him.

"Evelyn wanted me to advise you about a change she has made in her Will," Kevin started, leaning forward to pull out a stack of papers from his briefcase.

"Discussing her Will while she's here with us is unnecessary and insensitive. The last thing she needs is you drumming up more billable hours with unnecessary house calls," Michael retorted sharply, his mind racing with worry for his grandma. The Will was the last thing on his mind; he couldn't bear the thought of losing her.

Finding the section he wanted to discuss in the document, Kevin continued as if Michael hadn't interrupted. He cleared his throat and began reading, "To my grandson, Michael Theodore Cavanaugh, I bequeath the family farm of 30,000 acres of land, 17 outbuildings, and the main homestead, including all of the personal items found in the home and on the property in its entirety.

"However, because this is a family farm, it is only proper that Michael inherit it with his own family, to wit, his wife and/or children of his own issue.

"If, at the time of my death, Michael is unmarried, then the land will revert to the county to be made a proper wildlife refuge held in trust for all time. All of the bank accounts associated with this property, valued as of this date at $2.78 billion dollars, will also be held in trust for the maintenance of the land as a wildlife refuge."

As the words sank into Michael's numb brain, anger surged within him at the injustice of this new clause in the Will. Throughout his life, his grandma had promised him the farm, knowing it had been the only sanctuary he'd known during his troubled childhood.

"I can't believe this, Grandma! You know how I feel about marriage," Michael protested vehemently, his voice tinged with frustration.

Michael's heart pounded with indignation. He had no intention of getting married just to secure the farm, but he couldn't bear the thought of losing the place he called home to strangers. He needed time to think, to find a solution, and to fight for what he believed was rightfully his.

"Yes, Mikey. I've heard your grumblings about marriage more times than I care to count," his grandma replied calmly. "But it's time for you to set aside your hurt and pride and let someone into your heart. The right woman will make you into the man you were always meant to be."

Her words stung him to the core, reopening wounds he thought had healed long ago. Fear and uncertainty crept into his voice as he asked, "Aren't you proud of me the way I am?"

Feeling doubly betrayed, Michael couldn't believe his beloved grandma would speak to him like this. Maybe the disease was already affecting her mental capacities, and it filled him with anger and desperation. Dementia was one of the final symptoms to develop in cases such as hers. He was prepared to fight this new addendum, even if it meant declaring her with diminished capacity.

"Yes, Mikey, you've always been the perfect grandson," she replied, her tone unwavering. "And before you get any ideas that I'm getting soft in the head, I know exactly what I'm doing. I want to ensure you're taken care of before I meet my maker. Besides, it's high time you start thinking about making me a great-grandma, just in case I decide to kick this

Parkinson's in the butt." Evelyn reached over with her free hand and patted the back of Michael's hand where he still held onto her.

A fresh wave of guilt washed over him as she seemed to read his thoughts. How could he refuse her plea? If the idea of him getting married and having children could give her hope and incentive to live, then he'd have to put aside his reservations and give marriage a try. But the memory of his failed relationships, especially his last one with Angelica, made him hesitant.

His track record was pretty bad. He had no idea how to find the perfect partner.

Reluctantly, Michael realized he had no choice but to appease his grandma's wishes. The thought of losing the family farm to the Public Lands Division made his blood boil and fueled his determination to find a solution, even if it meant stepping into a world of uncertainty and taking another chance on love.

Probably just what his grandma had in mind when she put in the provision.

His grandma's underhanded tactic impressed and frustrated him simultaneously. He couldn't deny the guilt weighing on him as her condition loomed in his mind.

"I don't even know where to start," Michael lamented under his breath, the weight of the responsibility heavy on his shoulders.

To his surprise, his grandma heard him. "Start closest to home. You know, people you work with. Surely there're some good girls who understand real estate. As soon as you open your eyes, you'll start to notice how the girls look at you when you walk past. It's time you got your head out of your bank account and started listening to your heart's call for love."

Embarrassment washed over him again, knowing that the looks he received were often connected to his wealth, not his character. He didn't want a relationship built on material possessions; his failed experience with Angelica had taught him that. It made him feel dirty.

He struggled to keep his composure, resisting the urge to roll his eyes at her advice. His heart was just fine the way it was, unattached and free from complications. He had no intention of being bossed around or giving up his independence. As far as he was concerned, his life was already perfect – no attachments, no distractions, and most importantly, no disappointments.

However, the gravity of his grandma's request couldn't be ignored. He would do anything to make her happy, but the task ahead seemed monumental.

Forgetting entirely about the harbinger of bad news sitting across the room from him, Michael's mind raced through this latest task.

Determined to face it like a business transaction, he realized he had six months to find the perfect bride and secure the family farm. Maybe if he viewed it from a pragmatic standpoint, it would give his grandma the will to live even longer. After all, she never mentioned anything about love or longevity in her demand.

If you enjoyed this sample, Properties of Love is available now.

Get My Free Book Now

To let others know how much you enjoyed this book, please
leave a review at your favorite retailer.
To keep updated on upcoming books, visit
www.amyproebstel.com.
Receive a FREE book,
A Billionaire's Patent for Love
by signing up for Amy Proebstel's newsletter.
You can also follow Amy Proebstel on Facebook at
www.facebook.com/ATwistOnReality

About the Author

Amy is a *USA Today* bestselling author who writes sweet romance and young adult medical romance.

When she's not busy writing about endearing heroes, scheming villains, and Lone Star love stories, she spends her time binge-watching Hallmark movies, taking her husband and daughter flying (but not in the jets her billionaire's fly), playing with her Pomeranian and Pomskies, and cats, or reading.

A.B. Proebstel is the sweet romance pen name for Amy Proebstel, who also writes progression fantasy, epic dragon fantasy, and paranormal romance books that add a little magic to the world.

Please sign up for Amy's fantasy or romance newsletters on

her website at www.AmyProebstel.com or click Follow on her bio to get notices and updates when she releases new books!

- Get a bonus scene from A Cowboy's Recipe for Romance: https://geni.us/B1-ACRFR-Bonus

- Join her mailing list: https://geni.us/CleanRomance

- Join her Facebook group: facebook.com/ATwistOnReality

- Visit her website: amyproebstel.com

- Follow her on X: https://geni.us/Amy-T

- Follow her on Instagram: instagram.com/amyproebstel

She loves hearing from her readers.

Also By
Amy Proebstel

Billionaire's Bet, A Sweet Romance Series

Sweet Creek Ranch, A Sweet Romance Series

Wolf Shifters of Catskill County, A Fated Mate Shifter Series

The Chosen, A Fantasy & Magic Adventure Series

Dragon's Magic: An Epic Dragon Fantasy Series

The Rift in Our Reality, A Young Adult Medical Romance